TIME HUNTER

THE CLOCKWORK WOMAN

TIME HUNTER

THE CLOCKWORK WOMAN
by CLAIRE BOTT

TELOS
.CO.UK

First published in England in 2004 by Telos Publishing Ltd
61 Elgar Avenue, Tolworth, Surrey, KT5 9JP, England • www.telos.co.uk

Telos Publishing Ltd values feedback. Please e-mail us with any comments you
may have about this book to: feedback@telos.co.uk

ISBN: 1-903889-39-1 (paperback)
The Clockwork Woman © 2004 Claire Bott
ISBN: 1-903889-40-5 (deluxe hardback)
The Clockwork Woman © 2004 Claire Bott
Time Hunter format © 2003/4 Telos Publishing Ltd. Honoré Lechasseur and
Emily Blandish created by Daniel O'Mahony
The moral rights of the author have been asserted.

Typeset by TTA Press
5 Martins Lane, Witcham, Ely, Cambs, CB6 2LB, England • www.ttapress.com

Printed in India • Hardback edition bound in the UK by Antony Rowe Ltd

2 3 4 5 6 7 8 9 10 11 12 13 14 15

TIME HUNTER

Honoré Lechasseur and Emily Blandish . . . Honoré is a black American ex-GI, now living in London, 1950, working sometimes as a private detective, sometimes as a 'fixer', or spiv. Now life has a new purpose for him as he has discovered that he is a time-sensitive. In theory, this attribute, as well as affording him a low-level perception of the fabric of time itself, gives him the ability to sense the whole timeline of any person with whom he comes into contact. He just has to learn how to master it.

Emily is a strange young woman whom Honoré has taken under his wing. She is suffering from amnesia, and so knows little of her own background. She comes from a time in Earth's far future, one of a small minority of people known as time channellers, who have developed the ability to make jumps through time using mental powers so highly evolved that they could almost be mistaken for magic. They cannot do this alone, however. In order to achieve a time-jump, a time channeller must connect with a time-sensitive.

When Honoré and Emily connect, the adventures begin.

DEDICATION

For my parents, who are, without doubt, the two best, wittiest, kindest and most loving people in this or any other space-time continuum.

'She was created to be the toy of man, his rattle, and it must jingle in his ears, whenever, dismissing reason, he chooses to be amused.'
~ *A Vindication of the Rights of Woman* by Mary Wollstonecraft

The man and the girl walk through the streets, jostled by the passing crowds. They do not speak, knowing each other well enough to be comfortable with silence. It is a day like any other.

And yet . . . something is wrong. The man feels a faint sense of unease, an unplacable disquiet. He twists his head from side to side, trying to find its source.

There. That woman, the one in the blue coat. Her life . . . feels wrong. Different.

The girl is looking up at him now, confused by his behaviour. 'Honoré?' she asks, then again, 'Honoré? What's the matter?'

He shakes his head, as though trying to clear it. 'Her life,' he mutters, 'It's the wrong shape, Emily. The wrong shape . . .'

The woman turns, as though she has heard him. Looks him in the face. Seems startled, as if she recognises him. Opens her mouth to speak.

And her life rushes into his head like an express train, all muddled and far too long and the wrong shape . . . He stumbles. Catches the girl's hand.

– Timeslip –

When I hold my hand close to my ear and move my fingers, I can hear the whirring of tiny cogs. My eyes are enamel and ivory, overlaid on steel. My skin is carefully painted silk. I am, in short, a mechanical woman, cunningly made and perfect in every detail.

For a long time, I did not think there was anything strange in this.

After all, I was surrounded by similar mechanical contraptions; the squat, androgynous maid who dressed me in the mornings; the housekeeper who squatted in its bare, empty room, and could be communicated with through the speaking tubes in the corridors; and, of course, the attack dogs.

I was just one of these marvellous contraptions, set aside from them only by being the most extraordinary, the finest and most exquisitely made. I knew this was so, because Sir Edward Fanshawe had told me it was. Sir Edward would come to me from ume to time, undress me or tell me to undress myself, and require me to perform certain acts. I would comply, deftly, competently, and without any emotion or physical sensation at all. I have no sense of touch, you see. Sir Edward did not think it necessary to provide me with one.

Afterwards, he would lie beside me, stroking my long, dark hair that had been bought in a shop and attached to my head with strong glue, and murmur how marvellous I was – the greatest of all his creations, bar none.

When Sir Edward was otherwise engaged – in his workshop or his library, or tinkering with the glider up on the roof – I would usually sit in one of the window-seats and stare blankly at the view, or pace the corridors, my skirts swishing quietly along the carpet. I cannot say I was unhappy, but neither was I happy – nor angry, nor restless, nor fulfilled. I simply was. I suppose I must have felt contentment, for certainly I made no attempt to change my life.

I remember the day it all changed. The day the strangers came.

I was in the library with Sir Edward, re-lacing my bodice and adjusting the disarray of my hair, when the speaking-tube above the doorway coughed into life.

'The attack dogs have captured intruders, Sir Edward,' reported the gruff voice of the housekeeper. 'What should be done with them?'

Sir Edward sat bolt upright. 'Have them brought here,' he snapped. 'I shall deal with them personally.' He was furious, I could see; and with reason. Had he not told me many times that he had secluded himself in his family's ancestral home precisely to avoid the impertinent attentions of the kind of ill-educated numbskulls who had once plagued his youth? And so far, his efforts had been successful; so much so, in fact, that I had never seen any living human but him.

When the attack dogs (walking on their hind-legs, with their claws extended to grip the intruders by the arms) brought them in, I looked at them with interest. There were two of them: a tall, dark-skinned man in a long, leather coat and a slim, frail-looking dark-haired girl. That was amazing in itself. I had not been aware there were men who were not Sir Edward, or women who were not me. But the thing that made my cogs whirr a little faster was not that. It was the evident fact that these two had no cogs at all. I listened intently when the attack dogs marched them in, but I could hear not the faintest sound of machinery that didn't come from the dogs themselves; and I knew their sounds well enough, after many years. They were people of skin and bone and muscle and blood – like Sir Edward was. Until I saw them, I had thought, if I thought at all, that Sir Edward was the only non-mechanical person in all the world.

Sir Edward did not share my interest. He only glowered at the pair, and demanded, 'Well? Have you anything to say for yourselves?'

'We didn't mean to trespass,' said the man. He had a surprisingly gentle voice for one who looked so hardened and battle-ready, and a soft drawl to his tones. 'We're here by mistake. If you'd just let us go – '

'You're lying! You came to spy, didn't you? You wanted the secret of my devices! Well, you're not getting them, do you hear?'

'Like I said . . . ' the man began mildly, but Sir Edward had worked himself into a passion now, and was listening to no-one.

'Put them in the old wine-cellar!' he stormed. 'They'll see how we treat spies! Put them in there and lock the door!'

'Hey, wait a minute!' the man protested; but the attack dogs were already hustling him and the girl out of the door. As they passed, the girl (who had been standing with her head bowed, frowning as though she was trying to work something out) suddenly looked up at me. I saw a flash of surprise cross her face, and she opened her mouth, as if she would have said something to me. But the dogs did not pause, and she had no chance to say a word before the door slammed shut behind the intruders, and they were gone. Sir Edward snorted, and left the library, heading in the direction of his workshop, doubtless to calm his troubled nerves by working on one of his projects. I was left sitting where I was, staring at the closed library door. These people, that I had seen so briefly, were going to be put in the old wine-cellar, which had walls and floor and ceiling of stone, and a door of strong, thick wood. Sir Edward had made no provision for feeding them. They would die – and I had never even spoken to them! And the girl; she had looked at me, and wanted to speak to me. What might she have said? I felt I could not bear never to know.

I should make it clear that I did not, at that point, care about them for their own sakes; only for mine, that I would never get to speak to these, the first two real, breathing humans I had seen, other than Sir Edward. But why did I want to speak to them at all? I was built to serve Sir Edward, and I had never needed any other purpose to my life before. Perhaps I had already started to malfunction, even then; perhaps their arrival, breaking in on the smooth rhythm of my days and nights and days, had shaken loose some bolt, slipped some vital cog.

In any case, I found myself reasoning that there could be nothing wrong with going down to the old wine-cellar, only to listen at the door. Sir Edward had said nothing about my not listening to them, had, in fact, given no orders to me on the matter at all. Telling myself this, I slipped out of the library and, glancing swiftly in both directions to ensure that the dogs were truly gone, crept down the stairs. Down to where the wine-cellar was.

In the gloom by the door, I stopped, and bent my head closer.

'I think you're right,' the man was saying. 'It looked like the same woman – but how could anyone live so long – or be so unchanged? She looked the same age, exactly the same age! And you say you think we're . . . when? Early 19th Century?'

The girl answered, speaking too quietly for me to make out the words. Frustrated, I stepped closer. My shoe scraped against the flagstones as I moved, and both voices fell abruptly silent.

I craned my ear to the door, and a voice – the man's voice – right on the other side of it, said gently, 'Is there someone there?'

I answered without thinking. 'Yes. I am.'

'Who are you?' asked the girl. She too had moved closer to the door, for her voice came louder than before.

An easy question. 'I am Sir Edward's possession.'

'You're the woman from the library, aren't you?' the man said. 'What's your name?'

'Name?' I faltered.

'Yes, your name. Who are you?'

I wrenched myself away from the door. The question had set something in motion within me. I walked quickly away, up the stairs, back to my seat in the library, where I sank down in confusion. *Name?* Why should I have a name? Sir Edward had one, but that was different. The housekeeper had none, nor did any of the attack dogs, nor the maids. It made no sense for me to have a name. But then, why did it suddenly distress me not to have one, when I had never so much as thought about it before? The man had sounded so certain, so sure that I was going to be able to give him an answer, as though names were things that people *ought* to have. That *I* ought to have. But then, why had Sir Edward never given me one? Why had – no! I would not criticise Sir Edward, not even in thought. It was wrong to do so, it was wicked. I would not do so, nor would I go back down to the cellar. I would stay up here. I was not in the least curious about them, not any more. I had no desire to go down there again. None at all. None. I was quite content.

My conviction lasted two hours before I went down to the cellar again. I stood in front of the door, and rested my forehead against the wood. Inside, they were talking.

'But why won't it work?' the man was saying. 'Why can't we just time-jump out of here?'

'I think you need a timeline to read,' the girl replied. 'And we know you can't seem to read mine.'

There was a pause, then the man said, 'I guess we'll just have to hope that she lets us out, then.'

'But do you think she'll come back, Honoré?' the girl asked.

'I hope so, Emily,' the man answered.

So, they had names then. *Honoré. Emily.* But who was the 'she' they were talking about, the one who might come back? After a moment, it dawned on me that they were talking about me. I was pleased – unreasoningly, ridiculously pleased. So much so that I called out to them.

'I did come back,' I whispered loudly. 'I'm here.'

I heard footsteps stride quickly across the room, and Honoré said, quietly, 'We're glad you did. Now, will you let us out?'

'No,' I replied simply.

'Why not?'

'Sir Edward ordered you locked up. It was his express wish.'

'And can't you go against his "express wish", then?'

'No,' I said. 'He built me that way.'

There was a moment's silence. Then Emily whispered, 'He *built* you?'

The man named Honoré murmured, 'Sweet Jesus.'

'But what did he build you *for*?' Emily asked.

I began to tell her; but she interrupted after the first sentence, saying quickly, 'Yes. All right. I understand now.' There was a short silence, then she murmured, 'Good God, how . . . how degrading. Poor girl.'

'But what an amazing engineer that guy must be,' breathed Honoré, 'To build something like that. In an age like this.'

'"That"? Honoré, she's right outside the door, she can hear you!'

'Emily, don't you see, it's just a robot – a machine. It's got no feelings to hurt. It's only there to take instructions. In fact – hey, you out there!'

'Yes?'

'Let us out. Open this door, and let us out.'

'I cannot.'

'Look, I'm giving you an order – a direct order, don't you understand?'

'Why are you so angry?' I cried, stepping back from the door. 'Why are you angry with me? Are you angry with the lock, for keeping you in? With the door, for being what it is? I am Sir Edward's possession – nothing more! Let me be what I am.' I turned and fled up the stairs, my hands over my ears to shut out the sound of Honoré's voice calling me back.

That night, I sat in a padded window-seat in the library, looking out into the night. Needing no sleep, I usually spent the hours of darkness watching the moon slowly rise and set. But this night, it had scarcely cleared the horizon before I found myself growing restless, and realised I could sit still no longer. I rose to my feet, gathered my skirts into my hands, and set off through the sleeping house. The corridors were silent, save for the rustling of my skirts and the faint humming of my gears. When I passed a window, the moon peeped in at me as though wondering what I was doing – I, who was always so serene, now pacing the corridors in the middle of the night because I simply could not sit still. And indeed, I was wondering myself. This, I think, was when I first began to suspect I was malfunctioning. What part had gone wrong, I wondered, to make me feel so strange? Would I need to be mended?

Lost in my own thoughts, I didn't realise I was heading for the housekeeper's room until I stood on the threshold. I hesitated there a moment, then opened the door and slipped inside.

It was a large, bare room, and sitting in the middle of it was the housekeeper, a huge, fat cylinder of metal with pipes springing out at all angles and a dull red pilot light glowing at its apex, like a malevolent eye. The maids were lined up against the walls, silent, dormant, waiting to be called into action. I felt oddly vulnerable, standing in the house-keeper's own room – I had been here only once or twice before, and then only for a moment. But I knew that the housekeeper was not aware of me. It could see or hear only through the maids and the attack dogs; and the maids in here were all turned off.

After a moment, the uneasiness left me, to be replaced by an odd sense of glee. How strange it felt, and yet how wonderful, to be in the housekeeper's room in the middle of the night. I had never been forbidden to be there, so I was not doing anything wrong, but certainly I was behaving unusually. I had never behaved unusually before, had not realised how enjoyable it could be. I began to walk around the room, reaching out a finger every now and then to lightly touch one of the static maids. It was, as I have said, a bare room, and had only one thing in it that could have been in any way regarded as decoration. This was a hook jammed into the wall, at a height at which the maids could easily reach it. On the hook was hung a large ring, from which there dangled the keys to all the doors in the house.

My circuit of the room had brought me to stand directly in front of this hook. Now, staring at it, I began to tremble. Indeed I must be malfunctioning, I felt, for I had never trembled so before. Surely something was wrong, for my hand seemed to move without my willing it, to reach up of its own accord and grasp the ring of keys.

I stood there for a long time, holding on to the ring as though it was the only thing supporting me, staring at the keys. Then, slowly, I lifted the ring free of the hook, and drew it towards me. Clasping it with both hands, I hurried out of the room.

I had done nothing I had been forbidden to do, nothing that was against Sir Edward's instructions. He had never said that I was not to remove the key-ring from the housekeeper's room, never told me I must not carry it down the stairs, never ordered me not to stand in front of the old wine-cellar door, holding the ring of keys and shaking so hard I could barely stand. Never told me not to. Never said anything to the contrary. Never. I had done nothing wrong.

So far.

I could hear the sound of voices coming from within. Quietly, carefully, not wanting to slip again and let them know I was there, I moved closer.

'Anyhow,' Honoré was saying, 'that explains her longevity.'

'Maybe it also explains the strangeness you sensed in her timeline?' suggested Emily

'Maybe . . . but I think there was more to it than that. Something about the events in it. It seemed . . . important, somehow.'

'Perhaps, if she comes back, you'll get a better chance to look at it, and we can find out more?'

'I'm not sure I *want* to find out more. I just want to get out of here.'

'Well, you'd better hope she *does* come back, or we may never be able to.'

I did not understand the things of which they spoke. More than that, there was something about the manner in which they spoke that was utterly unfamiliar to me. It was as though it were possible for a man and a woman to converse, and to be in company, without giving so much as a thought to the kind of acts that Sir Edward desired me to do.. I had not known, until I heard them, that such a thing was indeed possible; but I knew it then. And I wanted to know more.

I managed to move my hand. The keys were still clasped to my chest. I selected the correct one, and began to bring it slowly down towards the lock. By the time it was level, my hands were shaking so hard that I needed to use both of them to push it in. I turned the key. The door swung open – only a little, but it was enough. I heard an exclamation from inside the cellar, and footsteps coming closer. Then they came out into the corridor – the dark-skinned man and the frail-looking girl. I would have spoken to them then; but my sense of my own wickedness, my base treachery, in releasing them against Sir Edward's wishes, overcame me so that it was all I could do to keep myself from sinking to the floor.

The man, Honoré Lechasseur, as I later discovered, turned, and saw me standing there. He held out his hand. 'Come here,' he said; and though his voice was soft, this was without doubt an instruction. Trembling still, I went over to where he stood, and gave him my hand. For a moment, he stood holding it, and I began to wonder if perhaps I should now begin to remove my clothes; but then he gave a small cry, and the darkness of his skin became ashy.

'Emily,' he whispered, turning to her. 'It's gone!'

She looked at him in alarm. 'The thing you felt? The important thing?'

'No, no, not that; her whole *timeline* has gone. It – it just stops, little more than a year from now.'

They looked at each other, grim-faced.

'Well,' Emily said, after a moment. 'That's that, then. We've got to stay, now.'

Lechasseur heaved a sigh so deep it seemed to have come from his boot-soles. 'I guess you're right. We've got no choice – until we can find some other way back to our time.' He glanced around, nervously. 'But we can sure as hell get out of this house.' He looked directly at me. 'How do we get to the grounds?'

I shook my head. 'Not the grounds. Dogs. The roof. That way.'

'Why, what's on the roof?'

'You'll see,' I managed. 'This way. Hurry.'

We crept through the stillness, up stairs and along corridors, past the library, past the dining-hall, past Sir Edward's bedroom (how I shook then!), past his workroom. Now I could see the door to the roof at the end of the corridor. In a moment we would be on the roof, and then they would go. And my days and nights would return to the same smooth, unhurried rhythm that I had known before they arrived. I would –

'*Stop!*' screamed a voice from behind us, and we turned in shock.

Sir Edward stood at the other end of the corridor, and his face was mottled with rage.

I closed my eyes. I remember thinking, clearly and calmly, 'This is the end. He will dismantle me and melt down my parts for scrap.'

I heard Sir Edward sneer, 'Trying to steal my toy, were you?'

Then it occurred to me that Lechasseur was still holding me by the arm to keep me from falling, and that although I still had the key-ring, the hand in which I grasped it was hidden in the voluminous folds of my skirt. I swung round as though trying to free myself, and surreptitiously pushed the keys into Lechasseur's hand. Turning my head slightly, I whispered: 'The door at the end of the corridor. Go!' Then I pulled myself free, and ran the few steps between me and Sir Edward to fling myself into his arms. I had done what I could, I had done everything I could, and it was up to them now.

Sir Edward caught me awkwardly, and I clung to him, impeding his movements, keeping him from running after Lechasseur and Emily, who were pelting down the corridor. Furiously, he shoved me to one side, and ran to the speaking-tube set into the corridor wall. 'Attack dogs!' he roared. 'Attack dogs to the roof, *now!*'

'They will be with you shortly, Sir,' replied the impassive voice of the housekeeper. Sir Edward snorted violently, and ran towards the door to the roof – it was open now, the key-ring still dangling from the lock. I gathered my skirts in my hands and followed him.

Out on the roof, the glider sat, quiet and serene, its nose pointing towards the dark sky. Its massive wings spread out from either side, and the cockpit . . . was empty.

In another moment, I saw why, and could have groaned my foolishness. There was only room for one person in there – I had not thought, had never before had to think, about the practicalities of escape. I had only remembered the glider, built to fly, and made for it blindly. Now I saw that the two fugitives were standing only feet from it, arguing fiercely. Of course – neither one would want to stay and be trapped; they would be fighting over their one chance to escape this place. But I could hear, faintly behind me, the howls of the attack dogs as they made their way through the house, and I knew that soon neither would be able to get away.

Then I saw Lechasseur grab Emily by the arm and push her – not away from the glider, but *towards* it. '*Get in!*' he shouted, loud enough for me to hear all the way across the roof. '*Now!*'

She did, then turned to look back at him. 'For goodness sake, be *careful*,' she said, hurriedly.

He took her hand in his own for a brief moment. 'You bet. Now *go*.'

Emily pulled the release lever, and the glider began to move along the launch tracks. Sir Edward, watching, gave a shriek of rage. 'My dogs!' he screamed. 'Where are my dogs?'

The glider picked up speed, moving across the roof, sliding smoothly past Sir Edward (who shook in impotent rage), and dropping neatly from the edge of the building to arc cleanly into the sky, under the moonlight.

She was gone, she was safe, the glider would carry her far away before it came to ground.

And the attack dogs burst onto the roof. It seemed to me, in that moment, that I had never really seen them before, only let my gaze slide over them, taking them for granted. Never seen how the light shone in long flakes from their metal sides, how their mouths snarled terribly and their teeth were like long knives. I looked at Lechasseur, and saw him drop into a fighting crouch. They were tearing across the roof towards him now. I buried my face in Sir Edward's shoulder. This I could not watch.

There was a short cry, quickly cut off, and I shivered in Sir Edward's arms. It was over. I should have rejoiced that I could return to the untroubled existence I had once known, but something in me seemed to revolt at the thought. I looked up at Sir Edward, and saw the glee on his face. I could almost have trembled again, the way he looked at me.

'Silly idiot jumped!' he exclaimed exultantly. 'Jumped off the roof. He'll be spread across the ground like butter now. Smack!'

Strange that, having known Lechasseur for less than a day, I should have so quickly begun thinking of his actions in terms of plans, of stratagems. Strange that a shred of hope leapt in me at Sir Edward's words. Gently, I disengaged myself from him, and walked casually to the edge of the roof.

Lechasseur, hanging by his fingers from a windowsill two stories down, looked up and winked at me.

'Is it a pretty sight?' came Sir Edward's voice from behind me. 'The body of a dead man – does it excite you, my little angel?' His footsteps came closer. He was going to join me on the edge of the roof.

I should have taken him by the hand, and drawn him to where I stood. I should have pointed down, and said, 'There is your enemy.' For a moment, I hesitated. Sir Edward was close behind me.

I turned, and stepped into his arms. 'Oh, it does, Sir. So much so, that I can barely contain my ardour. Will you join me in my rooms?' I drew him away from the edge of the roof as I spoke. I could feel myself shaking again, but he must have thought it was an excess of passion, for he only clasped me closer.

'I will join you in a moment. I have just a few things I need to put in order in my workshop – I was disturbed in the middle of an important construction.'

I led him towards the stairs. 'I hope it was not damaged by being abandoned?'

'Not at all. I must just complete a minor task before I can fully relax.'

'Then I shall wait for you with eager anticipation.'

We parted at the foot of the stairs, he towards the workshop, I in the direction of my rooms. But only until Sir Edward was out of sight. Then I took my skirts in both hands and ran towards that window, two stories down from the roof.

A foot away from it, I stopped, and leaned back against the wall. I was shaking, still. This was wrong, doubly and triply wrong. I should never have helped the two fugitives to escape, should not have concealed from Sir Edward that Lechasseur had survived. I was malfunctioning terribly.

I could still walk away. Lechasseur would lose his grip in the end, he would fall, all would be as it should have been.

No. I couldn't do that. I unlatched the window, and threw up the sash. My hands were trembling violently. I felt sure that if I reached out to help Lechasseur in, I would lose my hold on him and let him fall. I gripped the window-frame hard. I would not shake, I would be steady. I listened to the faint, gentle hum of my whirring cogs until the sound calmed me. If I was to malfunction, if it was inevitable, I would at least do it efficiently. The same way I did everything else.

I leaned out, took hold of Lechasseur's wrists, and hauled him inside.

'You took your time,' he grumbled, brushing himself down.

I motioned him to be quiet. Sir Edward might be listening. Beckoning Lechasseur to follow me, I led him down the corridor towards my rooms.

Once there, I felt a little safer. The familiar furnishings, the deep-pile carpet, the double bed strewn with cushions, all calmed me. I looked over at Lechasseur, who was examining a vase on the mantelshelf.

'This is really old,' he said, curiously fascinated. 'I can sense it. It comes from China, doesn't it?'

'I don't know. I don't know anything about vases.'

'Yeah, that's right, you're a robot. You don't know anything about anything, do you?'

I sat down on the bed, and picked up one of the cushions. 'Only one thing.'

He barely glanced at me as he set the vase back on the shelf. 'Oh yeah, I remember. You ≗ mentioned that.'

I might have asked him what he meant, if I hadn't heard footsteps approaching down the corridor outside. 'Quick!' I hissed. 'Hide!'

'Where?'

I pointed to the wardrobe. 'In there! Quickly!'

He darted inside, just as Sir Edward opened the door and came in. I hastily lay back on the bed, arranging myself into an alluring pose. Sir Edward locked the door behind him, then sat down and, without saying a word, reached for the ties of my bodice. I sighed in apparent ecstasy, and began to remove his breeches.

Later, I was lying with my head pillowed on Sir Edward's chest while he stroked my hair.

'That was even better than usual,' he said quietly.

'Yes,' I murmured, 'I felt it too.' Need I remind my reader that I had no sense of touch, and that Sir Edward, who had built me, knew this better than anyone? Yet he still liked to have me say such things to him.

'You are so marvellous,' he whispered. 'So very marvellous. And I made you. Who do you obey?'

'Only you, Sir Edward.'

He smiled at me. 'Only me. Always me. That's right.' He was silent for a long moment. 'You would never laugh at me, would you, my sweet?'

'Never.'

'Nor call me a fool for spending my days in my workshop.'

'You are a genius, Sir Edward. Of course you must spend your days in your workshop.'

He touched his lips to my hair. 'What would they say, I wonder,' he said quietly, 'if they could see me now?'

I did not know, I had never known, who 'they' were. But I knew from long experience what I must say now. 'They would envy you bitterly, and beg you to forgive them for their jeers and harsh words in the days of your youth.'

'Yes, they would. They would.'

'Of course they would,' I said, and reached out to touch Sir Edward in the ways that pleased him. He lay in murmurous pleasure for a moment, then sat up and looked down at me.

'This is a special occasion. You shall wear one of your special outfits, for me.' He got to his feet, pulling on his breeches, and went to open the wardrobe door.

I lay on the bed, watching. What else could I do? Never, in all my existence, had I attempted to deny him anything. Even to want to deny his desires was a thing from which my mind shrank, appalled. So I lay and watched, while Sir Edward opened the wardrobe door.

Lechasseur stepped out of the cabinet, as calmly as a man coming out of his own house. 'Hi there,' he said, urbanely, smiling at Sir Edward in a friendly way. 'As I said before, I really don't want to be intruding on your privacy. But I just had to meet you. You see, I'm Honoré Lechasseur, an officer in the US Army Corps of Engineers.' He paused, as though waiting for the other man to reply

Sir Edward was still looking at him, his mouth fallen open, his face a mask of utter astonishment. He made a few strangled sounds, but seemed to be otherwise incapable of speech.

Lechasseur leaned closer to him, and took him confidentially by the arm. 'We're really very interested in the work that you've been doing here – and particularly in your machine over there.' He nodded towards me, where I lay on the bed.

Sir Edward, completely taken in by this appeal to his pride, looked from me to Lechasseur, and I saw an almost painful hope begin to grow in his eyes. 'You – you understand? You see how – what an achievement, what a vast achievement – '

'Sure,' Lechasseur replied, soothingly. 'We understand these things. From what we hear, you must be the world's greatest inventor.'

Sir Edward turned to face him, his eyes positively glowing with delight. 'Oh I am!' he cried. 'I *am*! My dear sir – will it please you to follow me? I would like to show you,' and here his voice dropped a tone, becoming low and confiding, 'my *workshop*.'

Lechasseur looked deeply gratified. 'That would be a privilege, indeed.'

Sir Edward turned to me. 'Dress yourself, my dear. You shall come with us.'

I began to put my clothes on as quickly as I could, my mind in a whirl. The US Army Corps of Engineers? Was that really where Lechasseur had come from? But then, why had he not said so straight away? Had he perhaps thought that he would be treated as a spy? Or was this all simply a ruse to deceive Sir Edward? If so – I glanced quickly at Sir Edward while I dressed – it was certainly succeeding. So taken was he with the idea of being visited by a representative of a foreign power, that he had not even questioned why such a man would be hiding in his wardrobe. I laced up my bodice and slipped on my shoes, then turned back to the men. 'I am ready, Sir Edward.'

'Now, sir,' said my master, taking my arm, 'follow me.'

As we went down the corridor, I kept my eyes on my shoes, trying to prevent my excitement and trepidation from showing. For I had never seen Sir Edward's workshop before; nor, I believe, would I have seen it now, if not for the fact that my creator wanted to show off his other inventions without relinquishing the chance to show off my own wonderful beauty. Yes, I knew I was beautiful – how could I not? I had been told so many times.

Now we were at the door of the workshop. There was a moment's pause while Sir Edward fumbled in his pocket for the key; then the lock clicked open, and he ushered Lechasseur and me inside.

It was a marvellous place. There were shelves around the walls, piled high with all manner of mechanical parts, besides other things; fur, wool, silk, glass, coils of gold wire, piles of semi-precious stones. And on the work-benches around the room stood marvels.

One of these, the nearest, was a perfect facsimile of a small, lithe black cat, crouched down and looking for all the world as though it were about to spring. This Sir Edward took up in his hands, and turned over and over as he stood addressing Lechasseur. 'Now, you will, of course, have heard of Vaucansen?'

'Of course,' Lechasseur replied. 'Who hasn't?'

'Indeed, sir, indeed! Who has not heard of him – amateur though he is, bungler though he is, who has not heard of Vaucansen? And yet I, who have long worked in utter seclusion, have produced far more wondrous things than he. Take his famous duck, for example. Does it resemble a duck? Is it feathered? Does it quack? Does it splash through puddles seeking worms? No! It eats grain, and it flaps its wings. Oh, and it excretes, apparently, or performs a pretence of that act, but I for one am perfectly convinced that that pretence is a fraud, sir. The man is a fraudster! Now, take my cat, here – look at my wonderful cat, and tell me, if you will: is it not superior to any *defecating duck*?' With that explosion of utter scorn, Sir Edward put the cat back on the work-bench, then tugged hard on the whiskers to the right of its mouth. Immediately, it rose from its crouching position, looked around at the three of us, and blinked. Then it sat down in the middle of the workbench and began to wash itself. Sir Edward virtually crowed with glee. 'You see? You see?'

'Impressive,' agreed Lechasseur.

'And there is more!' Sir Edward raised his hand, as though he would strike the animal, and cried in a warning voice, 'Scat!' The creature instantly crouched once more, ears back, and hissed angrily at its creator. But he, with a swift motion, took hold of the whiskers to the left of its mouth, and tugged them. Instantly, the animal was still and lifeless once more. Sir Edward turned to Lechasseur with a broad smile on his face.

'Truly amazing,' the tall man replied.

'Ah, but I can do better than that – much better. And have done! My dear sir, my most brilliant creation is standing before you!' With that, he took me by the hand, and drew me forwards. 'Now, sir, having heard of Vaucansen, you will of course know what a ridiculous fuss was made of his two human-like automata?'

'Sure.'

'Well, they are nothing, nothing, compared with her. She is a walking miracle. Every part of her – Take, for instance, her pubic part, which I have made to tighten around the member by an extension of the well-understood principle of the uneven cam – but you would not believe, my dear sir, the sweetness of the sensation as she tightens and loosens – I have even added a modification to make her speed her operation as climax is neared – ' He broke off suddenly, and put his hand on Lechasseur's arm. 'My dear sir,' he said, in a voice trembling with emotion, 'would you like to have it demonstrated? Would you like to experience this marvel, this miracle, for yourself? You are the first human being who has ever offered me understanding – I would offer you something in return. My dear sir – my dear friend – I would offer you the greatest thing I could offer any man. You may experience my beauty, my angel, for yourself.'

Lechasseur lifted Sir Edward's hand away. 'Thanks. I appreciate the offer. But I think I'll pass.'

Sir Edward stared at him, his face a mask of incomprehension. 'You – you decline?'

Lechasseur seemed embarrassed. 'Well,' he mumbled, 'it is only a machine.'

'A *machine*?' Sir Edward's face was suffused with sudden rage. 'My greatest creation – my dearest, my darling – a machine?'

'Well, yeah, like you said yourself.' Lechasseur was calm, his voice pitched at a tone clearly intended to soothe. But his words were anything but soothing to Sir Edward, who abruptly turned and punched him hard in the stomach.

Lechasseur doubled over for a moment, then straightened up, gasping a little. 'Hey, look now – ' he began, but Sir Edward flew at him before he could finish, and he was forced to put up a defence.

They fought. I watched as they did so, my hands at my lips to keep myself from shrieking, my emotions in such turmoil that I could not have said who I feared for most – Sir Edward, Lechasseur, or myself. Sir Edward was a heavily-built man, but Lechasseur was younger and tougher, and seemed able to fend off or dodge his blows with relative ease. I could see Sir Edward growing angrier and angrier – and he had been angry enough to begin with.

Then, as Lechasseur passed by where I stood, Sir Edward called out to me. 'Stick out your foot!' he shouted, and I did. What else should I have done? He was my master.

Lechasseur tripped and fell. Sir Edward was on him in a moment, locking his hands around his throat, tightening. Lechasseur grabbed at Sir Edward's wrists, trying to pull his hands away, but Sir Edward was determined, and now it was strength against strength. I sank on to a nearby bench, my hands at my lips. I watched. I did nothing. Lechasseur's hands weakened, fell aside. I saw his eyes begin to flutter closed.

No!

I thought I had shrieked aloud, but Sir Edward never glanced at me. And then I knew that it was only inside my mind that I had cried out, only inside my body that

No! reverberated through every section, every part, turning me into nothing more than one shuddering denial that staggered up, took a spanner from a nearby workbench and cracked a blow across the back of Sir Edward's head.

I was sitting on a bench. On a bench, in the workshop. Sir Edward sprawled at my feet. Not moving. Chest rising and falling. Asleep. Wake up, Sir Edward. Wake up and tell me what to do. Wake up. Let me please you. I live to please you. To do the things you tell me to. I'll never do anything else. Never. Wake up.

Someone shouting. Saying something. About leaving. Strange thing to say. Why would I leave? Sir Edward is here. I am waiting for him to wake. Where would I go? There is nowhere for me but here.

'Tell me the way out!'

An order. I obey orders, I am good. 'Down the stairs. Turn right through the hall.'

Someone pulling me to my feet, out of the door. Where are they taking me? I want to stay with Sir Edward. Surely he will wake soon. I would resist. But I don't know how to. It is not part of my design. Down the stairs. Right through the hall. Are we going outside? I have never been outside. Please, don't make me go there.

The fear of outside pressed in on me, dragging me back from my entranced state. I was being led through the hall by Lechasseur. Sir Edward was . . . my mind shied away. Best not to think about that. Just follow Lechasseur. Do what I'm told.

Then we stepped through the front door, and out into the night. Lechasseur hesitated a moment, and looked around. 'This way!'

'No!' I cried, terror of death bringing me back to myself; and I laid my hand on his sleeve to pull him back. A moment later, I recoiled, as though the leather of his coat had been red-hot metal. I had been bad, had tried to tell him what to do. Now he would be angry, terribly angry with me.

But he only turned, and asked quickly, 'Why not?'

'That is the wrong way,' I stammered. 'We must get to the gate as quickly as possible, or the dogs will take us.' My days of watching the gardens had paid off, and my memories of the layout were intact.

He nodded curtly. 'You're right. Which way to the gate?'

I pointed. He set off quickly, calling, 'Come on!' over his shoulder. For a moment, I stood hesitating on the doorstep. I could go back inside, back to Sir Edward. If I was lucky, he would not remember that I had hit him, only that he had fought the interloper. Perhaps he would think that the interloper had struck him down. I could tell him so. I could go back to the life I had had before the strangers came. Quiet. Peaceful. Uneventful.

Or I could follow Lechasseur. He was making for the gate. Planning to leave. I could go with him. Explore places I had never even thought of. Leave the estate. Leave Sir Edward.

Lechasseur was almost lost to sight amid the undergrowth. I had to choose now. With a low moan, I stepped away from the door, and walked hurriedly after him.

I caught up with him quickly, and together we plunged through the bushes of the overgrown, untended estate. Dry twigs and rotten branches cracked under our feet, leaves showered down on us like an early autumn. We could not have gone quietly, even if our situation had been less urgent. All too soon, I heard the attack dogs baying in the distance.

'They are coming,' I whispered.

'What are?'

'The dogs. They are coming after us.'

Lechasseur glanced at me. 'Can you run?'

'I don't know. I have never tried.'

'Try now,' he said grimly.

We ran.

Faint and far-off, I could hear the attack dogs crashing through the undergrowth. Maybe we would have time to reach the gate. Maybe. We ran side by side, matching each other's pace. To my surprise, I found that I could run. I ran well, even, with long, clean strides, hardly breaking step to leap over a fallen branch in our path. The same well-wrought cogs that had allowed my legs to curl so seductively around Sir Edward's waist drove me swiftly through the woods on the day I ran away from him. But the attack dogs were behind us, and gaining.

'There!' shouted Lechasseur, and I saw the thing he pointed to – a large, tumbledown barn standing solitary in the middle of the woods. We ran to it, dashed inside, slammed the door. Lechasseur seized an old plank lying on the floor, and jammed it against the closed door.

'That will not hold them for long,' I said.

But Lechasseur was staring at something over my shoulder, not listening. I turned, and saw, in the moonlight that fell through the cracks in the walls of the barn, a white, horned horse, standing perfectly still with its head raised. It seemed to shine in the moonlight, and, had I been in the habit of breathing, it would have taken my breath away. Until that moment, my own face in the mirror had been the most beautiful thing I had ever seen. Now, I saw beauty bodied forth in a form entirely unlike my own, and was stuck dumb by the marvel of it.

'A unicorn!' said Lechasseur. And then, a moment later, 'But unicorns are only a myth. What the – ?' He approached it cautiously, but it made no movement at all as he drew closer. Finally, he touched its flank with one hand, and still it was motionless. 'Of course,' he murmured, 'it must be another of his machines. Broken, though.' He drummed his fingers on the unicorn's hide, thinking. 'I wonder if I can get at the mechanism somehow,' he murmured, more to himself than to me.

I shook my head in despair. 'You could not mend that! It is only Sir Edward who can create or mend the devices.'

He glanced at me. 'Oh, I wouldn't be so sure. I know a thing or two about engines. Okay, I never was in the Corps of Engineers like I said, but I've been a lot of things in my time, including a mechanic.'

Close to, one of the dogs howled. 'You will need to be very fast indeed,' I said under my breath. But Lechasseur had already lighted on some tools that Sir Edward had left by the unicorn, evidently abandoned in a huff when he had failed to rectify whatever was amiss with it. Now he ran his fingers lightly over the unmoving beast's hide, giving a faint exclamation when he found a small catch that enabled him to open a panel in its flank.

'There! Now, they reckon adrenalin concentrates the mind, don't they? I guess we'll find out if they're right.'

Outside, I heard the triumphant bay of an attack dog, and a moment later something slammed against the door. I sank down upon a box that had been abandoned there. The dogs had found us. I felt myself growing faint, and recalled, in the middle of the clamour and yelping that rose from the pack outside, that I had omitted to wind myself the night before. In sudden terror lest my mechanism should run down entirely, I drew out the key that hung on a slim chain around my neck, and inserted it carefully into the small hole concealed in the roof of my mouth. One – two – three – four – five twists of the key, and I was wound up again for another day, or two – depending on how much energy I should use in that time. Or (I thought, as the door shuddered under the impact of the dogs) on whether or not I would be torn to pieces long before my works had a chance to even begin to run down.

'Almost done,' Lechasseur said briskly, as another thud shook the building. 'Nearly ready now – there!'

The unicorn tossed its mane and neighed, Lechasseur straightened up with a pleased smile – and the attack dogs burst through the door. Lechasseur sprang onto the back of the unicorn, holding out his hand. I grasped it, and was pulled up to sit behind him. The dogs charged at us, baying hate. The unicorn wheeled, lashing out at them with its hooves, almost throwing me off.

'Hold tight!' shouted Lechasseur. I clung to his waist and buried my face in the back of his coat. He drove his heels into the beast's flanks, operating controls placed there, and the unicorn leapt forwards, over the dogs, out of the door of the barn. Through the woods we rode, the dogs pursuing. But now they began to fall behind – fleet though they were, the unicorn was faster, and we rode swiftly on while the baying grew faint behind us. I raised my head to look back, and saw no sign of them. But my attention was arrested and held by another thing – the brightness of the stars, and how clear the sky was, how clean and pure the air. All around us lay the woods of Sir Edward's estate, and, for a moment, the wildness of it – so different from the tame, ordered world I had been used to – almost frightened me. But then the moment passed, and I felt only exhilaration; at the woods around us, at the sky above, and at the glorious speed with which we were borne on our way. I had never ridden anything before, had not known what a wild joy it could be.

Soon we were at the gate and the unicorn cantered to a halt. Within, Sir Edward's estate; beyond, the world. All the things I had never seen. I had read the books in the library; but all Sir Edward's books were scientific. I could have expounded the principles of physics, if I had ever been called upon to do so; but I knew nothing at all about what the world looked like.

Lechasseur rose to stand on the unicorn's back for a moment, then leapt, caught hold of the wrought-iron decorations at the gate's top, and swung himself over.

I hesitated a moment, but my decision had been made. There could be no turning back now, with the attack dogs slavering behind me. Rising to my feet on the unicorn's back, I flung myself upwards, and a moment later dropped to the ground on the other side of the gate.

Pale light shone down on Lechasseur and me as we left the estate behind us and set off across the downs. The moon was high in the sky now, the night was much advanced. We reached the top of a small eminence, and paused a moment.

The land was spread out before us, more space than I had ever seen in my life before. It frightened me. So much emptiness. The only thing that arrested the eye was a small huddle of houses down in the valley.

'We should make for the village,' Lechasseur told me. 'We might be able to find shelter there.'

I nodded, and followed him.

'Honoré,' I said, as we descended the hill, 'Where does the world stop?'

'Stop?'

'Yes; where does it end? Where is the boundary?'

'Well, there really isn't one, in that sense.'

'You mean – it is infinite?'

'No, it's round.'

None of Sir Edward's books had ever mentioned anything like this; they were for advanced men, not schoolboys, and assumed a great deal of knowledge that I simply did not have. I was intrigued. 'A sphere? What keeps things from dropping off the bottom of it?'

He looked a little annoyed. 'Do you always ask this many questions?'

I shook my head. 'I never have before.'

'Then why now?'

'Because – because it is all so new!' I looked around, marvelling at the space that surrounded me. A thought struck me. 'Honoré, how many other mechanical people are there in this world?'

He paused, then said quietly, 'I guess you're probably the only one.'

That brought me up short. 'No others in all the world?'

'Yes.'

We walked on in silence. I do not know what Lechasseur's thoughts were, but mine were not happy. I was alone in the world. There was no-one else like me. I could almost have turned and run back to Sir Edward's estate. What was the use of a new world, if there was no-one out there who could truly be a companion to me?

'I do not want to be all alone,' I said out loud.

Lechasseur shrugged. 'You'll get used to it.'

I glanced at him. The words sounded insensitive, but there was a rueful undertone to them. 'Are you, then, alone?'

'You ask too many questions,' he said; and would say no more.

For a while we walked with silence between us, but my curiosity would not be held in for long. Finally, I burst out with the one thing I wanted to know most of all. 'Honoré, why did I – do what I did?'

'What do you mean?'

'Well, why did I –' I shuddered, then forced myself to be still. 'Why did I strike him, Honoré? Sir Edward – why did I strike him?'

He frowned at me. 'Well, how do you expect me to know?'

'But you understand machines, do you not?'

'Yes.'

'Then – should you not understand me?'

He gave me no answer, but walked on in silence, and would no longer meet my eye.

I looked about me as we walked. *This is the world*, I said to myself. *This is the world, and it is far, far greater than I had thought it. My world was carpeted corridors, still rooms, the view from a window.* For the first time, I allowed myself to feel a pang of distaste for Sir Edward. He had known that this world, this glorious place, was out here, and he had made no attempt to show it to me. Nor, now that I came to think of it, had he done anything at all with the aim of pleasing me. It had been his pleasure, his happiness, that had been the important things; and I had been nothing to him. In my mind, I turned away from his image. *I can live without you*, I said to it silently. *I can, and I will.*

Eventually, we reached the village, and walked through the darkened streets. There was only one point of light. As we came towards it, we saw that it was a large building, the doors and windows open to the warm summer night, golden light spilling out of them along with the sounds of laughter, conversation, enjoyment. It was an inn, the first I had ever seen. I would have shrunk back, afraid of so many people, but Lechasseur walked briskly to the door, and I followed.

Inside, the noise was even greater, the lights brighter than they had seemed outside. At the opening of the door, everyone in the bar glanced up briefly; and remained frozen, staring at the pair of us. The noise died. Innocent that I was, this reaction bewildered me. It was only later that I discovered that a man with dark skin is not welcome everywhere, and that this is particularly so among the ill-educated and the un-travelled. Assailed by a barrage of hostile stares, we made our way through the crowd to the bar at the back of the room.

There was a tall, lugubrious-faced man standing behind the bar, but he looked studiously away from us, as though he had not seen us come in; though I knew full well that he had.

Lechasseur leaned forwards to get his attention. 'We need a room for the night.'

'Not sellin' nothin' to no Blackamoor without cash down,' the man snapped, still not looking at us.

Lechasseur reached for his pocket, then suddenly stopped. 'Ah . . . I guess I don't actually have any of your kind of money.'

'Well then you can bloody well get out, you and your heathen ways. Or if yer won't get out, move away from the bar so decent Christian folk can get served.'

We stepped to one side, and Lechasseur looked at me with a frown creasing his brow. 'Damn. We could really use a room. We need to rest, or I do, anyhow.'

I looked around the bar. Most of the patrons were still watching us closely, though pretending not to. After a moment, I began to notice a difference between the way they looked at Lechasseur and the way they looked at me. For Lechasseur, their expressions held suspicion, tinged with more than a little fear When they turned their attention to me, I saw a gleam in their eyes that I recognised from long experience. Even if everything else was new and strange, there was one thing in this place that was familiar; desire. I understood desire. I knew what to do with it.

I looked about until I saw a well-dressed young man on his own. He looked more prosperous than most of the others there – perhaps the son of some local land-owner. Casually, I turned away from him, back towards the bar.

'Honoré,' I said quietly, 'would you go over and sit by the fire, and try to look as though you have nothing to do with me?'

He stared at me. 'What?'

'Listen,' I said, not looking at him, 'Do you remember when I told you that I only knew about one thing? This is the thing I know about. Trust me, Honoré, please. Have I betrayed you yet?'

He hesitated a moment, then shrugged and did as I asked. I waited a moment, then went over to where the young man was sitting in the corner.

'May I join your table?' I asked.

He smiled broadly. 'Certainly. My name is Adam. What is yours?'

I looked around the room in a panic. Behind the bar, I caught a glimpse of a stuffed white bird in a glass case, its wings outspread as though for flight. I turned back to Adam. 'Dove. My name is Dove.'

He reached across the table to take my hand. 'A beautiful name for a beautiful woman.'

Sir Edward, when he was in the mood for a slightly more exotic enjoyment even than the one I usually offered him, would often have me play out scenes for him. Whore and Customer was one of them. So I knew the things I should say, the poses I should take up. I knew them as well as I knew my own hands.

Lowering my gaze with a flutter of lashes, I murmured, 'You are bold, sir.'

'And yet, I notice you do not draw back.'

I looked up again, meeting his eyes briefly. 'No, sir. I am not noted for drawing back.'

'Tell me, what are you doing in this place? We do not often see – women such as you.'

'I have had to leave my home town, due to scandal. I am travelling.'

'And do you have a place to stay, tonight?'

I shook my head. 'No, sir.'

'Perhaps you would care to share a room with me?'

'Perhaps I would. For a while. How would you persuade me to?'

He shifted deliberately on his stool. I heard the chink of a well-filled purse, and nodded. 'Indeed, a most excellent persuasion. Shall we retire, sir?'

For answer, he rose to his feet and went over to the bar. I saw money change hands, and then he came back over to me. 'Will you come up to the room I have arranged for us, lovely Dove?'

I followed him up the stairs.

Afterwards, I lay beside Adam while he counted coins into my hand. I looked at them as he did so, marvelling at the solid chink of them. I had never earned money before. The fantasy of Whore and Customer had always ended before the payment part was reached. But now, I had earned money. By my actions – the same actions that I had performed for Sir Edward, with no wage at all – I had won these bright coins in my hand. I folded my fingers closed on them.

'Thank you, sir,' I said.

He shook his head. 'Thank *you*. That was – amazing.'

We lay a moment in silence, then he rose and dressed. 'I must get back. My mother will worry.'

'And she would be right to,' I murmured. He laughed. 'As you pass through the barroom,' I added, 'Could you tell the man I came in with to come up to this room?'

'Assuredly. Is he your bawd?'

I knew enough, from the games I had played with Sir Edward, to understand that word, and I knew enough of Lechasseur to know how far it was from anything he was, or ever could be. But, after all, how could I explain to Adam what the truth was? 'Yes,' I said, 'He is my bawd.'

Adam grinned, and left the room.

I rose and dressed. I was re-lacing my bodice when I heard footsteps on the stairs, and a moment later Lechasseur entered.

'I have a name, now,' I said to him. 'I chose it myself. My name is Dove.'

He nodded curtly, and went over to the window, where he stood looking out.

I tried again. 'Dove is who I am, Honoré. I decided on that name. It is my name, now. I chose it.'

Still he said nothing.

'Honoré?'

'That young guy *leered* at me,' he said, not turning, in tones of suppressed outrage. He sounded angrier over that than he had over being locked in a cellar to starve.

I felt a moment's remorse. I should not have told Adam that Lechasseur was my bawd; I ought to have foreseen that this kind of misunderstanding might occur. Then, unexpectedly, I felt a fire of anger begin to stir in me.

'You are ungrateful, Honoré,' I said quietly, 'You have not thanked me for securing you this room. Nor have you said one word of thanks to me for saving your life, not on any of the three occasions when I did so.'

He did not turn from the window. 'No. I suppose I haven't.'

I clenched my fists. 'Say thank you to me, Honoré, or I will have you turned out of *my* room.'

Now he did face me. 'You can't order me about like that.'

'Why not?'

'Well, you're a – ' He hesitated.

'A what?'

He was silent.

'Honoré! *What am I?* I – I would like to know.'

'Frankly,' he burst out, 'so would I. You're supposed to be a machine, but you don't talk like one, you don't act like one –' He broke off in frustration.

'So – you do not know.'

'No. I don't.' I could see the admission cost him something.

I hesitated a moment, then impulsively drew out the small key that hung on a chain around my neck. 'Do you see this?'

He nodded.

'I have a small hole concealed in the roof of my mouth. Every few days, I wind myself up. That is all. I am clockwork. And perhaps that is the answer to your questions, and to mine – that I am clockwork, and nothing more.' I concealed the key once more in my bodice, and made to turn away.

'Dove?'

I looked back.

'Thank you,' Lechasseur said softly.

I gave him the money I had earned, so that he could go down and buy himself food in the taproom. When he came up again, I said, 'You may have the bed. I do not sleep, in any case.'

He shrugged. 'If you want. Like you said, it's your room.' He began to prepare for bed.

'Honoré,' I said suddenly, 'where is Emily?'

He glanced at me. 'I don't know.'

I sat down on the bed. 'But – she will be all right, will she not?'

He shrugged. 'I don't know. I think so. I hope so. She's a resourceful young woman. But . . . ' his voice trailed to a halt.

I looked up at him. 'You like her, do you not?'

He nodded. 'Yes. We're friends.'

'Honoré, please tell me, what is liking like?'

He looked at me curiously, then slowly sat down beside me on the bed. 'You really don't know, do you?'

'I do not. All I know is the acts Sir Edward used to ask of me.'

Lechasseur looked at me for a moment longer, then turned his eyes away, and began to speak. 'Liking . . . well, its about . . . being concerned for a person. Wanting to have that person around because . . . well, you're happier if they are. But really, right deep down, it's about caring. And Dove,' he turned to me again, 'you *do* know about that. Or why else would you have let Emily and me out of the cellar?'

'I . . . I wanted you to be alive. To stay alive. Not to be hurt.'

'Exactly.'

'But I didn't even know you then.'

'It's not just about the people you know. Caring – is about everybody. Everybody who needs to be helped. Even if it hurts you, even if you get into trouble, you've got to do something if someone else is in danger. You can't just sit by while people are getting hurt, or might be or will be hurt. You have to take part in life, or you aren't really alive.'

When Lechasseur had fallen asleep, I found myself growing restless. The old, placid nights of watching the moon rise and set had left me forever, it seemed. I left the room, and descended to the taproom, which was dark and empty, stools stacked neatly on tables. I crept to the door, unlatched it, and stepped out onto the street.

Outside, it was a wild night, small clouds scudding across the moon. I wished I could feel the wind against my face. Even seeing the effects of it was glorious. I stretched out my arms in mute obeisance to the night.

'Dove, is it?' said a voice at my back, and I turned, startled. Behind me stood a young man, whom I recognised as having been in the taproom that evening. Like Adam, he was better dressed than most. Unlike him, he did not have the look of a local. He seemed like a man who belonged somewhere other than here. 'I saw you descend the stairs, and thought I would follow you.'

'Do you come from these parts, sir?' I asked.

'No. I'm a London man, here for a holiday from my work. But you hardly seem to be a native, yourself.' He raised his brows, making the last sentence into a question.

I did not like him. There was something in his face that was obscurely distasteful. 'What I am or am not is my own business,' I said shortly, turning away from him.

He moved around me, so that we were again face to face. 'Ah, but I have a proposition for you. One that you might find interesting.'

I shrugged. 'What is it, then?'

He smiled, showing vulpine teeth. 'I have always harboured a desire to make love in a moving carriage. Tomorrow, the weekly coach arrives in the village. I will offer the coachman a great deal of money to depart from his usual course and take me for a short – but not too short – ride across the downs. I will offer you a great deal of money to accompany me.' He stepped back, and spread his hands.

I considered the offer. The small stock of coins that Adam had paid me was half exhausted from paying for Lechasseur's meal. Breakfast would leave us penniless. If we were to live, we must get money in some way. 'How much?' I asked.

He smiled 'Fifty pounds.'

I thought frantically. Was this a good offer? I remembered that Sir Edward had once shown me a fine gem that he had bought to use in manufacturing some automaton or other, and told me that it had cost him one hundred pounds.

'Is that a lot of money, Sir Edward?' I had asked him.

He had stroked my hair and smiled at me. 'It is a great deal of money, my darling.'

So, fifty pounds . . . half a hundred pounds . . . half a great deal of money . . . and the man, now that I looked at him, wore an expression that said as plainly as words could that he expected me to be pleased and astounded by the offer. So it probably was a good offer, even a generous offer. And we were in need of money . . .

'I accept,' I said.

He smiled his fox-like smile. 'Good. I'll meet you by the halting post at ten o'clock sharp.'

'Wait, sir,' I called, as he turned back towards the inn. 'You have not told me your name.'

'Haven't I? Well, it is Peter.' Then he was gone. I stood outside for a moment, then went in, my relish for the wild night diminished.

The next morning, I explained the situation to Lechasseur. He did not like the fact that I had agreed.

'Never mind about the money. What we need to do is to find Emily.'

I shook my head, exasperated. 'Very well. We shall think of a plan to do so. Will that please you? And do you object terribly if, in the meantime, I try to ensure that we – or, at any rate, you – do not starve to death while we come up with this plan?'

He sighed. 'All right. Let's go.'

When we arrived at the halting-post, Peter was already there, waiting. 'The coach will be along shortly, Dove. Does your companion wish to accompany us?'

Lechasseur glared at him, before turning on his heel and going to stand several paces away.

I smiled at Peter. 'No,' I said, 'he does not.'

We waited in silence for the coach. Soon we saw the cloud of dust in the distance that heralded its approach, then the coach itself rumbled into view. The coachman pulled up, stepped down from his box, and tied his horses to the post. Several people descended from the interior, and walked off down the street chattering excitedly. Peter stepped up to the coachman, and murmured in his ear. I saw the glint of money passing from hand to hand. The coachman looked up at me, then back at Peter. He seemed to be about to refuse, but Peter took him by the buttonhole and drew him closer, murmuring again in his ear. More money passed between them. Finally, the coachman nodded, and Peter beckoned me over.

'The deal is done, sweet Dove. Will you step inside?'

I took my leave of Lechasseur with a brief nod, and stepped up into the carriage. Peter stepped in after me, smiling like a fox.

Inside the carriage, Peter turned to me. 'Before we set off, there is one more thing that would vastly increase my enjoyment. Would you object to being bound?' He drew a stout length of rope from his pocket.

I hesitated.

'I will double the money I shall pay you,' Peter said tantalisingly.

I was very innocent then. I am wiser now, by dint of hard experience. If I had known . . . But I did not. I held out my wrists to him, and let him bind them. He tied the knot swiftly and deftly, then looked up at me, still smiling, holding my bound hands in his own.

'To London!' he shouted, and the coach took off with a jerk. I tried to pull away, but he held me tightly.

'London?' I cried. 'London was not in the bargain! Let me out – let me off!'

Peter only smiled more widely. 'London was not in the bargain I made with you. But it was the main part of the bargain I made with the driver. The other part being that he should not stop till we reached the city, save for to rest the horses. I told you that I was on holiday from my trade. I did not tell you what that trade was. I am a procurer for a London brothel, Dove. I was impressed by your openly displayed talents in the taproom last night, and so made the necessary steps to secure your services. We shall be in London by sunset.'

I sank back against the seat, overcome. At a stroke, I was on my own again. It was a dreadful thought. If, at that moment, I could have returned to Sir Edward's estate, never to leave again, I would have done so gladly.

The coach rattled on. Peter released my hands after a while, but kept a firm hold on the skirt of my gown. I stared out of the window, sunk in apathy, and watched the countryside sweep past outside. Even in my present plight, I could not help noting how much, how very much of it there was. I had thought that the downs Lechasseur and I had walked over to reach the town had been large, but the country seemed to go on and on, with no end to it. For hours we drove, and still the landscape swept by serenely on either side. It made me quite dizzy to imagine the amount of space there must be. I tried not to think about it.

I am Dove, I said silently to myself. *My name is Dove.* It was something to cling to; I had a name, I knew who I was. Peter had called me by my name, and I had gone to him, and been trapped . . . *Names have power*, I thought. Other people could use them against you, or you could use them yourself . . . *I am Dove. My name is Dove.* It was a handle to cling to, now that all else was taken away.

Finally, when the sun was beginning to sink, we reached London. If I had been dizzy before, I reeled now. All the people! I had not thought there could be so many people. But here they were, all thronging the streets, pouring past the carriage on all sides.

This was the moment when I could have escaped. Peter still held my gown, it is true, but nevertheless I could have cried out, could have bawled that I was being kidnapped, abducted. Perhaps it would not have helped me at all – but then, perhaps it would. Why, then, did I not call out? The simple answer is that I did not, in truth, wish to. After all, the duties of a brothel would not be onerous to me – there was nothing they could ask me to do that Sir Edward had not required of me a hundred times. And at least there I would be free of the need to care, to choose, to act, that had pressed in on me so hard since leaving Sir Edward's estate. Perhaps I could sink back into placidity, perhaps I would be able to go back to the way I had been before all this had started, before Lechasseur and Emily had come. So though I parted my lips a little, I made no sound; and the carriage arrived at the brothel door with no interference from me.

Peter hurried me in, and pushed the door shut behind us with his foot. There was a large, strong-looking man standing in the corridor, raising a slab-like eyebrow at the pair of us; and to him, Peter said, 'Fetch Bella, would you, Dan?'

The mountainous Dan rumbled an agreement, and lumbered off. Peter waited impatiently, clutching my arm, until a stout, blowsy woman waddled into view at the end of the corridor. 'Bella!' he greeted her. 'See what I've brought you!'

She came closer, and looked me up and down. 'I do see. Petey, don't yer ever rest? Yer supposed to be on 'oliday, and 'ere you 'ave sent me two already.'

He nudged her jocularly in the ribs with his elbow, clearly in high good humour. 'When I see an opportunity, Bella, I take it. And this was an opportunity not to be missed!'

Bella – a strange name for a woman so unbeautiful! – looked me over once more. 'Very nice indeed, Petey, but where do I put 'er? The other one took up me last spare room.'

He shrugged indifferently. 'Put them in together then.'

'I suppose I shall 'ave to. Dan!'

The mountain-man appeared at the end of the corridor, and came over to our little group by the door.

'Dan, take this lady up and put 'er in with the other one.'

Peter's grip on my wrist tightened. 'Money first, Bella.' His tones, that had been so jocular, had turned suddenly soft and icy.

Bella sighed and rolled her eyes. 'Really, Petey, don't yer trust me?'

'Frankly, no.'

'Oh, all right then, here's yer money!' She fumbled at a purse that hung from her belt, drawing forth several large coins and shoving them into Peter's hand. 'Now will yer let Dan take 'er?' she inquired sarcastically.

Peter let go of me, and bowed with an exaggerated flourish. 'By all means.'

Dan wrapped his huge fingers around my arm, and half-led, half-dragged me along the corridor and up the stairs at the end of it. At the top of the stairs was another corridor, this one with doors running along either side of it. At the very end of the corridor, Dan stopped and rummaged in his pocket for a moment, before pulling out a key, unlocking one of the doors, thrusting me through and shutting the door behind me. I heard the sound of the key turning again in the lock.

At the other end of the room, a woman stood, her head bowed, looking down through the barred window at the street outside. For some reason, she seemed oddly familiar –

In another moment, I knew. You will think that I ought to have been overcome with relief, that I should have been glad that I was not, after all, alone. I regret to say that my first feeling was one of sudden anger. I had been anticipating a quiet life, doing the things I had done many times before, not thinking, not caring. Now that was snatched away, for here was someone I knew, who had already proved her ability to disrupt my life; had I not lost everything when I had rescued her and her friend? Now that I had found, it seemed, a place where I could come to a halt once more, would she take this from me, too? But then she began to turn, and I saw the confusion and fear in her face. My anger was swept away by a flood of concern. Bitterly ashamed of my feelings of but a moment ago, I hurried across the room to her and caught both her hands in mine. 'Emily, it *is* you! But how did you come here?'

She shook her head, clearly bewildered by my sudden appearance. 'I don't know. I crashed that glider thing, knocked myself out, and woke up here.'

'I suspect,' I said darkly, remembering the conversation I had overheard downstairs, 'that Peter had something to do with it.'

I later discovered that my supposition was correct, and that Peter had stumbled across the crashed glider and had then hired a farm-hand and his hay-cart to make the journey with Emily, bamboozling the man's simple wits with a trumped-up tale of a sister prone to madness and fainting fits, and of a London sanatorium that was the only place that could effect a cure. But this is by the by.

'Peter?' Emily asked. 'Who's Peter?'

I shook my head. 'An unpleasant man. It does not matter.'

She shrugged, letting the subject drop. But a moment later I wished she had not, for the next question she asked was, 'What is this place, do you know?'

I would rather have answered a thousand questions about Peter than reply to that. I had not forgotten her reaction when she had asked me what I was made for, and I had begun to answer. But she had a right to an honest reply. 'A brothel,' I said softly. 'This is a brothel.'

For a moment, her face was shattered with horror. Then she clenched her fists, and hardened her features. 'If anyone comes near me,' she said in a voice that barely shook at all, 'they're going to regret it.'

I looked at her, and knew what would happen. I knew some things about brothels; Sir Edward enjoyed making them the settings of the little scenes he would sometimes have me act out. So I knew that, for a new young whore, one not used to the trade, there would be a time of 'training'. So it was called; but this was not the learning of skills. What it meant was that someone, a man employed by the house, would rape her, over and over again. There would be deliberate humiliation, meant to shatter her spirit. This would go on until they broke her.

Emily was strong, and would not break easily. Maybe she would never break, maybe she would die first. Perhaps she would kill herself, rather than suffer what she would have to suffer, here, in this house. In the back of my mind, a quiet voice said, *'You can't just sit by while people are getting hurt, or might be or will be hurt.'*

I dashed to the door, and pounded on it hard with both fists. There was no response. I hammered harder. Finally, Dan's voice said, 'Quiet in there!'

'I have a proposition for Madam Bella,' I said quickly, before he could leave. 'A business proposition, which will make her a great deal of money if she accepts. If she finds out you kept her from hearing about it, she will be very angry with you. Fetch her!'

There was a long silence; then I heard the floorboards creak as Dan walked away. I waited there, standing before the door, to find out whether he had gone for his mistress, or only shrugged and walked away.

'What are you doing?' Emily asked from behind me.

'Something that I hope will work,' I replied, without turning.

Finally, after what felt like an eternity, I heard footsteps ascending the stairs, and coming down the corridor towards our door. The key scraped in the lock, the door opened, and Bella stood there, with Dan looming behind her.

'Well?' she demanded. 'What do you 'ave to offer me?'

'Myself,' I said calmly. 'Or rather, my skills. I am not only beautiful, Madam Bella, I am very, very talented. I can do things to your gentleman visitors that will drive them near-insane, and make your brothel the most frequented, and the most expensive, in the whole of London. But this I will do only if you accede to my requests.'

'What requests?'

'Those I am about to put to you. First, I want three good, wholesome meals a day, and not laced with opium, either. Secondly, I want a hot bath brought up to my room every day before the gentlemen arrive, and I wish to be alone while I bathe. Thirdly, I want a maid. A personal maid, assigned to me alone. She must not be one of the girls of the house; I will not have my maidservant corrupted by sluttish tricks. Her only job must be to attend to my needs.'

Bella regarded me narrowly. 'If yer can do what yer say yer can do, the food and bath I can give yer easy. But maids is expensive.'

'No maid, no bargain.'

Bella considered this for a moment. Then, suddenly, she brightened. 'What about 'er?' she asked, pointing over my shoulder at Emily. 'Never been part of the house yet – new, yer see. She 'ull make yer a nice maid, I'll be bound. And if she ain't so clever at it, well, yer can always train 'er up.'

I nodded graciously. 'That would be acceptable.'

I thought I had succeeded, and was surprised to have found it so easy. But then Bella, leaning against the door-frame, asked shrewdly, 'But 'ow do I know yer as good as yer say yer are?'

'Can you risk dismissing the possibility?'

'Oh, I ain't going to turn yer down. But what I am going to do is make yer prove yerself. Dan, stay 'ere, and make sure these ladies stay 'ere too.'

She waddled off down the corridor. A short while later, she returned, towing Peter behind her. 'Do 'im,' she said. 'Do 'im for me, an' I shall watch. Then we shall see.'

It would be Peter, of course. And before them all, before Bella and Dan; and worst of all, before Emily. I did not look at her, I could not look at her. If I did, I would falter, and I could not afford to falter. Instead,

I smiled sweetly at Peter as though he were my closest friend in the world, and began to unlace my bodice.

Afterwards, when Peter had pulled on his breeches and stumbled, breathless and bow-legged, out of the door, Bella nodded to me. 'Yer on,' she said, and left the room without further comment, Dan following behind her.

I pulled on my dress again, and sat on the edge of the bed, smoothing my hair back into place. I heard footsteps behind me, and then the bed creaked as Emily sat down. She took my hand, and held it between both of hers. I looked up. I thought I saw tears in her eyes, but it might have been only a trick of the light.

'Thank you,' she said simply.

I smiled at her, then. 'You are very different from your friend.'

'My friend?'

'Honoré.'

Her hands tightened on mine. 'Honoré? How is he? Is he safe?'

'Quite safe, when last I saw him.'

'Where – no, start at the beginning. How did the two of you get away?'

I told her, in as few words as possible, the story of our escape and what had followed. When I had finished, she sat musing for a moment, then gave me a long look.

'You're a remarkable person, Dove.'

I raised my brows. 'Person?'

'Oh, don't talk that way! You *are* a person, I know that you are.'

I shrugged, uncomfortable with the turn the conversation had taken. I did not know quite *what* I was, and preferred not to think about it, if possible. In a clumsy attempt to introduce a new topic, I said abruptly, 'Where do you come from, Emily, you and Honoré?'

Her face became grave. 'That is two different questions, Dove.'

I frowned, confused. 'What do you mean?'

She looked away from me for a moment. 'I . . . am not from the same place and time as Honoré.'

'Place and *time*?' This was new to me. I had not known that travel through time was possible, and said so.

'Nor do most people.' She drew her hands away from me, and sat staring at them as though the answers to all the riddles of the world were written on their palms.

46

'How then do you travel? By what means? How did you come to Honoré's time, if you were not from there?'

She laughed in a way that was neither amused nor glad. 'I don't know.'

'I do not understand.'

'Neither do I. I . . . ' she gestured in a helpless way, then let her hand fall to her lap again. 'I have amnesia, Dove.'

I knew that word. I must have found it in my reading through Sir Edward's library. 'I'm so sorry,' I said, and I was. It must be awful, I thought, to have whole areas of your memory unavailable to you.

'I don't know who I am, Dove,' she said quietly, 'I just don't know. I know my name, and that's all.'

'A name is something valuable to know,' I offered, in an attempt to comfort her.

She shook her head. 'It's not *enough*. I can't remember my parents, my childhood, where I come from. I know I came through time and space, but I can't remember what happened. And I don't know *why*!' Her voice cracked on the final word. If I had had a heart, it would have broken for her then. Instead, I put my arms around her and drew her head down to lie against my shoulder. She wept very softly into my hair.

After a while, she squeezed my hand silently and sat up, pushed her hair back and became suddenly very businesslike. 'Right. The first thing we have to do is work out a way of getting out of here.'

I looked up at her wonderingly. The question of trying to escape had not even occurred to me.

'The bars on the window are padlocked from the outside,' she went on, 'so that's no use. The next time Dan comes in, one of us could distract him while the other slips past – '

'I do not think that Dan is very easy to distract, somehow.'

'All right, then, we could overpower him.'

I laughed outright at that. 'I doubt if Samson and Hercules, working together, could overpower him.'

'Well then, we could dodge past him.'

'How? He fills almost the whole doorway.'

'Yes, but he'll have to come all the way into the room at some point, won't he? To bring the baths and meals. We could try to escape then.'

I looked at her eager face, and sighed. 'If such an opportunity arises, then yes, I will try to escape with you.'

She left it at that.

The days went by, and no such opportunity arose. Emily, as my maid, fetched my (or rather, her) meals and baths herself, with Dan accompanying her every step of the way. She was turned out of my room while I was entertaining the guests, and sent to sit in Bella's tiny parlour, but again Dan accompanied her from and to my room. As for me, I was never allowed out of the room at all. I was far too valuable to Bella for that. We were, it seemed, caught fast.

I would be lying if I said I was dismayed by this. To tell the truth, I was happy. My duties were not onerous to me – there was nothing the gentlemen could ask me to do that Sir Edward had not required of me at some time – and Emily was there. For the first time in my life, I had a friend, and I revelled in it.

I was, as I have said, happy. But Emily was not. The confined nature of our lives told on her nerves, and the fact that we were dependent on our captors maddened her. There were other things, too, that distressed her. I found out about one of them after we had been several days in the brothel. It was after I had been entertaining one of the gentleman visitors. Dan escorted her back into my room, and closed the door on us. She walked past me without speaking, and went to stand by the window, looking down at the street.

'I saw that man on the stairs,' she said. 'The one who was – visiting you.'

'Did he look pleased?' I asked.

She snorted. 'Oh yes. Very happy.'

'Good.'

She rounded on me. 'Why is it good? Why do you do the things you do, just to make men like that happy? They aren't thinking of you as a person, you know, Dove – just as a – a kind of *thing*.'

I smoothed my skirts. 'Well, perhaps I am just a kind of thing.'

Emily stamped her foot. 'You are *not*! Don't say that about yourself, it's not true. You deserve better than all this!'

'But, Emily, all this is the only thing I know.'

'Then *learn something new*!' she cried, exasperated.

'Something – new?' I faltered. New was frightening, new was dangerous. Far better to stay with familiar things.

She sighed, and her gaze softened. Leaving the window, she walked across the room to me and put her hands on my shoulders. 'Dove, you do have a right to choose, you know. And if this was the life you'd chosen, I wouldn't say a word. But it's not. It's what you do because you've always done it, because it's what you were taught, because you think you don't have a choice. Well, you do. You could do something different if you wanted to.'

'But why would I want to? This life is familiar to me, and comfortable.'

Emily shook her head. 'If all you wanted was familiar, comfortable things, why didn't you stay on Sir Edward's estate when you had the chance?'

I struck her hands from my shoulders, and turned away. 'Why do you do this?' I cried. 'Why must you ask me questions that you know I cannot answer? Why must you keep making me *think*? I was content before you and Honoré came, I was safe!'

'Dove,' Emily said gently, 'were you happy?'

All the anger left me in a rush. I turned back, and met her steady gaze. 'No,' I said, 'I was not happy.'

It was several days after that that I first met Sir Richard. He was one of Bella's gentleman guests, and he bounded enthusiastically into the room; a tall, muscular fair-haired man, with a familiar glint in his eye when he looked at me.

'You must be the wondrous Dove that Bella has been telling me about. I am Sir Richard Hampden.'

I extended my hand. 'I am pleased to meet you, my Lord.'

He took my hand and bowed over it, brushing it with his lips. When he straightened up, there was a faint smile on his face. 'Indeed, a dainty morsel. The only introduction most whores seem to know is, "Lie down there while I take me drawers off."' He took a step back, and gazed at me. 'But you – ah, you are magnificent! A night with you would be a reward well worth having, indeed.'

I curtseyed demurely. 'Thank you, my Lord.'

He shook his head and laughed. 'Oh, don't thank me. Thank the one who sent you to me – as, indeed, I intend to, when I see him again.'

'And who might he be?' I asked, unconcerned as to which of my clients he had been speaking to.

Sir Richard's smile widened. 'Oh, a large man, sturdily built. And, by-the-by, a Blackamoor.'

My hands clenched into involuntary fists, and I stared at Richard in amazement. 'What did you say? Who – his name – tell me his name!'

'Honoré Lechasseur.'

I sat down heavily on the bed. 'You *do* know him.'

'I know him. He sent me to find you.' Sir Richard stood for a moment looking in my face, then shook his head in bewilderment. 'So, he is dear to you, then? Well, you amaze me. I never would have thought such a lovely woman would have been driven to find comfort in a Blackam – '

I shot to my feet. 'Do not call him that! Do not dare call him that!'

He shrugged. 'Why not. It is what he is, after all. A plain, descriptive term.'

'Not the way you say it. When you say it, it is an insult. A slur.'

'Oh, come now! I have no hatred for Blackamoors, and this one in particular I have a certain fondness for. Why, he is staying in my house, I am helping him look for you. Does that argue dislike?'

I shook my head. 'No; but you think him less than a man. I see it in the way you talk about him. Well, I tell you he is not. He is a better man than any I have met since.' I shot a pointed look at this Sir Richard.

The young man scowled, and turned the conversation. 'Well, in any case, I have been trying to find you for some time.'

'You have found me. What now?'

Sir Richard leaned closer. 'Now, we must find a way to get you away from here, and back to your friend.'

This, of course, was the moment when I could have demurred, could have said, 'I do not wish to leave with you. I would rather stay here.' I did hesitate a moment. But only one moment. Then, rising to my feet, I said quietly, 'The bars on the window are padlocked from the outside.'

He looked at the window, then back at me. He nodded. 'Stay awake this night, pretty Dove.' Well, that would be easy. He took my hand, and kissed it again. 'I take my leave of you.'

'Wait!' I said, as he turned away. 'Tell Honoré that Emily is here. Tell him she is unhurt.'

He raised his eyebrows. 'Who is Emily?'

'His friend.'

Sir Richard bowed. 'I shall tell him. Adieu, Dove, until we meet again.'

Then he was gone. I paced the room, waiting impatiently for Dan's heavy tread in the corridor outside, accompanied by Emily's lighter footsteps. Finally, I heard the floorboards creak, and a moment later Emily came in, looking puzzled.

'That didn't take very long,' she said, looking at me quizzically. 'Did he have a sudden attack of shyness?'

I took her hand and drew her away from the door, my finger to my lips. Together we waited in silence until we heard Dan move away from the door and down the stairs.

'That man was sent by Honoré,' I said.

She stared at me. 'Honoré? But – *how*?'

'I do not know. But I do not think he can be an impostor. I told him about the padlock on the window bars, and he said I was to remain awake tonight.'

'I'll stay awake with you.'

I smiled, and squeezed her hand affectionately. 'Dearest Emily, it is no hardship for me to watch through the night, while it would be one for you. You must sleep, or at any rate try to. Only, lie down fully clothed, so as to be ready for what might occur.'

She smiled. 'Are you sure you'll be all right keeping watch on your own?'

'Quite sure,' I said confidently. Emily gave me a look that could have been interpreted any number of ways, but acceded to my request and settled down to sleep at the appropriate time.

By the time midnight struck, I was a nervous wreck. Every carriage that rumbled past in the street, every sudden unheralded noise, made me start and wonder if this was the moment. Always it was not, and I settled to watch once more. And always the next sound startled me anew.

I rested my forehead against the glass of the window, and tried to relax. The moon shone down brightly outside, lighting up the street below. It seemed strange that the same moon that lit those London cobblestones had peered in at me through the windows of Sir Edward's house a lifetime ago.

Something large landed with a thud on the windowsill, and my view of the street was abruptly cut off. I leapt back, barely choking off the shriek that rose to my lips. A moment later I began to laugh shakily – for Lechasseur was crouched on the windowsill, grinning in at me. I darted across the room to the bed, and shook Emily gently out of her sleep. For a moment, she blinked at me, bewildered, then memory returned and she swung herself quickly to her feet.

Lechasseur had taken from his pocket something I now realise must have been a lockpick, and was tampering with the padlock. After a few minutes, he had it open, and pushed the bars aside. Then I drew up the sash, and Lechasseur dropped into the room. He had a rope tied about his waist, which he untied, and held out to Emily.

'Just get onto the windowsill and hold on tight,' he whispered. 'Richard will pull you up.' She scrambled out, and a moment later was hauled up out of sight. Then the rope was dropped down again. Lechasseur caught hold of it, and held it out to me.

I took it, and was hauled upwards.

As my head cleared the level of the roof, Emily reached out to heave me up. Sir Richard gave the rope one final tug, and through their combined efforts I landed safely on the rooftop. We lowered the rope one more time, and in another moment, Lechasseur was with us. Sir Richard caught me by the hand. 'Come on!' he whispered, and we ran.

We ran over the rooftops of London, the four of us, softly and swiftly in the chill of the night, scrambling past chimneys, leaping the gaps between buildings, the moonlight falling on us and the small sounds and smells of sleeping London drifting up to us as we went. And then it was a clamber down a sloping roof and a short drop to the ground, where Sir Richard's carriage was waiting in the gloom. Suddenly, as we began to move off, the wild glory of our escape, the joy of being among friends, all overwhelmed me, and I lay back against the cushions of the seat and laughed for pure happiness. Then Emily began to laugh as well, for the same reasonless reasons as I, and we shrieked with laughter like fishwives while Lechasseur and Sir Richard looked at us as though we had run mad.

'Well,' I said, finally, when the storm had subsided, 'we are much obliged to you gentlemen, much obliged indeed. But Honoré, I should like to know how you managed to arrive so opportunely. We certainly did not expect you.'

'It's a long story.'

I looked at the young nobleman. 'Sir Richard, is your house near here?'

He smiled. 'It is quite a distance, I should say.'

I turned back to Lechasseur. 'You see? We have all the time you could require. And if it is, as you say, a long tale, I am quite sure that it will nevertheless be an interesting one.'

He shrugged. 'Well, okay then.'

I settled myself against the cushions, and he began.

After the coach took off with me, Lechasseur, who had heard the cry 'To London!' and the beginnings of my indignant protest, chased down the road after us for a way. Then the coach began to pick up speed, and he abandoned the attempt as futile. Instead, he went back to the village, and asked the locals how he might get to London.

Why, by coach, they told him.

And when was the next coach due?

It was in a week's time. In any case, a moment's reflection reminded him that he had no money to pay the fare.

'Is there any other way I could get to London?'

'Walk,' they said.

So he began to walk.

He did not, then, know that Emily had been taken to London as well. The only thing he did know was that the journey to London would be arduous and uncomfortable, and possibly dangerous as well.

He tramped down the road for all the first half of the day, until the sun stood high in the sky. It was almost noon when he heard the sound of wheels behind him, and turned to see a waggoner driving slowly along the road. Struck by a thought, he hailed the man, who stopped.

'Aye, what is it you're wanting?'

'Are you going to London?'

The waggoner let out a deep, low laugh. 'To London? Nay, not so far. But I'm going along the road that way for a while. Hop up, if you want to!'

'I'm afraid I don't have any money,' Lechasseur said, climbing up to sit beside the man.

'Nay, I don't need thy money. Just glad to have a body to talk to.' Having said this, the man lapsed into silence. After a long while, he added, 'What takes you to London, then – a gen'leman like you, setting off wi'out money or a coach to carry you?'

'I'm going to find a friend.'

At that, a gleam lighted in the man's deep-set eyes. 'Ho yes? Lady friend?'

'Yes, actually.'

'Pretty, is she?'

Lechasseur considered this. 'Yes, I suppose she is.'

'*Ho* yes,' said the man with deep satisfaction, and gave another low, rolling laugh. After that, he fell silent again, rousing himself only at intervals to glance knowingly at Lechasseur, utter '*Ho* yes,' in pleased tones, and laugh to himself. Lechasseur bore this as well as he could, largely because he didn't think asking the man if he would kindly shut up would have done any good at all.

Finally, as the sun was beginning to sink, the man pulled his horse to a halt at a crossroads, and said, 'I'll be going this way. You need to turn that way, for the London road.'

'Thank you very much,' said Lechasseur, getting down.

'You're welcome, I'm sure.' Then he flicked his whip and was off, looking over his shoulder briefly to deliver one final, triumphant, '*Ho* yes!'

Lechasseur shrugged, and headed off down the London road. The sun was setting, making the clouds glow golden in a lilac sky. Slowly it sank below the horizon, reddening as it went, leaving the sky to fade into a deep, rich blue. The stars began to come out, pale pin-pricks of light.

Lechasseur trudged on through the night, while the slow stars wheeled above him. And when the first grey light of dawn began to smudge the sky, he stood on the brow of a hill, looking down at the city of London. But still there were many hours of walking before him; it was past noon by the time he was well in among the streets and byways of the city.

Tired, footsore, hungry, parched, and distracted by his concerns, Lechasseur paid little attention to his surroundings. Nor did he notice when he turned down a dead-end, until he looked up and saw the blank wall rising before him. A little annoyed, he turned to retrace his steps.

'Nah then,' said the largest of the three thugs who stood blocking his way. 'Give us yer money an' no-one gets 'urt.'

Lechasseur sighed. 'I don't have any money.'

The man sneered and spat. 'None o' that, Blackamoor, none o' that.

You're wearing a nice coat – yer can give us that for starters.'

Lechasseur took a step back, raising his hands in a conciliatory gesture. But the leader had balled his hands into fists and was stepping closer, followed by the other two. Lechasseur stepped back again and set his back against the wall, preparing to fight.

'Hey, you! What's going on here?'

The leader cast an unconcerned glance over his shoulder at the well-dressed young man advancing down the alley. He motioned to one of the other thugs. 'Jonny, sort 'im out.'

The one addressed turned and lumbered towards the young man, who took a pace back. 'Now, I would advise you to back off a little, I really would.'

'Oh yes?' grunted Jonny, raising his fist. 'Or what?'

The young man kidney-punched him, fast and hard. 'Or that, I'm afraid,' he said, as the unfortunate Jonny folded up.

Then things became a little interesting. It was three against two, but one of the three was winded and both of the two were good, experienced fighters. It wasn't long before the thugs fled in a body, leaving Lechasseur and the young man in possession of the field.

'Well, sir, a lucky meeting for you!' said the young man, in high good humour. 'My name is Hampden, Sir Richard Hampden.'

'Pleased to meet you. My name is HonorÈ Lechasseur.'

'And what were you doing here? This isn't a safe area simply to wander around in.'

'To tell you the truth, I got lost. What are you doing here yourself, if it's so dangerous?'

Richard grinned. 'Visiting a girl. A very pretty one. In any case, they know me round here, well enough to stay away – and they shall know to keep away from you in future, by Jove! That was well fought, well fought indeed. I should like to square up to you myself some day, in the boxing ring, if I ever had the opportunity.'

'Well, maybe some other time. Right now, I'm busy with something else.'

'Oh yes? What?'

'I'm looking for a friend of mine.'

Richard grinned broadly. 'A girl, is it?'

'Yes, as a matter of fact.'

'In that case,' Richard said, flinging his arm around Lechasseur's shoulders, 'You must tell me all about it. Come back to my house, we can talk there.'

' . . . and I'm worried what's happened to her,' Lechasseur explained, rather later, over whisky in Sir Richard's study.

Richard tapped his cigar into the grate. 'Pretty, was she?'

'I don't know why everyone keeps asking me that. Yes, she was. Is.'

'Well then, unless I miss my guess, she would have been taken to a brothel.'

'What!'

'Oh yes. Not all the girls in those places are there by choice, you know.'

'No, I shouldn't think they are.'

Richard took a long drag on his cigar, considering. 'Well, there's one very simple way of finding her. I'll just have to make some discreet inquiries and find out which of the brothels have acquired new girls in the past day or so.'

'And then?'

He tapped his ash into the fire again. 'And then, my dear Lechasseur, I shall have to find out which of the new arrivals is your friend Dove, using more . . . direct means. It shouldn't take me more than a week or so – I think I can probably manage at least one girl a night, don't you?'

'Well, I really don't think –' Lechasseur began.

Sir Richard lay back in his chair and laughed. 'Oh, you are a prude, Lechasseur. Luckily for you, I am anything but – despite what you may have heard about me. I'll find your friend for you. Just let me have my fun along the way, hey?'

Lechasseur sat back and regarded Sir Richard thoughtfully. 'What do you mean – despite what I may have heard about you?'

'My name means nothing to you?' asked Sir Richard, a pained expression on his face.

''Fraid not.'

'Why, sir, I am a Member of Parliament, and particularly noted, if I may say so, for my speeches about the sanctity of the family, the purity of a chaste woman.'

'I guess that makes you quite a hypocrite, doesn't it?'

Sir Richard leant forwards, his expression more serious than

Lechasseur had previously seen it. 'I cannot live this way all my life,' he said quietly. 'To be a debauchee at sixty would make a man ridiculous. And I do not care to sit by the fire and mumble over a pocketful of memories when I grow too old for gaming and whoring. I want to be somebody. A minister, perhaps even in the Cabinet. To stand a chance of reaching such a height, I have to espouse popular causes. And what could be more popular than the defence of home and family? It is a theme every Englishman can thrill to. But do not think me a hypocrite, Lechasseur. You seem a good man, and I should hate to have you think ill of me.'

Lechasseur shrugged, and turned the conversation to other topics.

By the time our carriage arrived at Richard's house, it was well past midnight. Lechasseur and Emily went yawning upstairs to the beds that had been prepared for them, leaving Richard and me alone in the library. He turned to me with a smile, and I knew the look in his eyes. Seeking to delay the inevitable, I turned aside and took up a book that was lying on a small table.

'*A Vindication of the Rights of Woman*, by Mary Wollstonecraft. Do you like this book, Sir Richard?'

'Oh! Lord no. Utter trash.' He took it from my hands, and threw it back down on the table. 'A pretty woman like you should not bother with rubbish such as that.'

'If you think it rubbish, why did you buy it?'

'Oh, I am working up a speech about the foul crowd of unnatural Amazons who seek to draw women out of their proper sphere. But why are we standing here talking? There are more interesting things we could be doing.' He caught me by the shoulders, and brought his mouth down upon mine. I stood passive, enduring his kiss, and thinking: he has not even asked me. He has assumed I will do what he wishes me to do. He has not even asked me if it is what I wish for too.

I did not know if he treated me this way because I had been a whore, or if he would have reacted to any pretty woman in the same manner. Whichever was the case, I found – somewhat to my surprise – that I was becoming angry. I put my hands up to Richard's chest, and gently pushed him away. 'Sir Richard – who am I?'

He looked down at me, bewildered. 'You are Dove.'

'And who is Dove?'

'Why, a remarkably pretty young woman.'

'And – what else?'

He laughed and shook his head. 'What else is needed?'

A kind of thing. I turned away abruptly. 'Good night, Sir Richard.'

He did not understand, but only took my hand in his and said, laughing, 'It will be a very good night, Dove, when you cease playing the fool and come upstairs.'

'But I am not playing the fool. And I shall not come upstairs.'

There was a long moment of silence, while I watched the bewilderment ebb slowly out of him, to be replaced by stubborn rage. 'And what makes you think,' he asked, his voice cold, 'that you have any choice in the matter?' He took a step towards me.

'The fact that if I shriek aloud, Emily and Lechasseur will be down here in less than a minute,' I replied, as calmly as I could. 'And I do not think that even you, Sir Richard, could complete your business in less time than that.'

He stood fuming for a minute, then turned on his heel and left the room without another word to me. I heard his footsteps retreating down the corridor, then silence. The kind of deep, velvet silence that descends only late in the night, when the darkness outside the gas-lit room seems to press in upon one like a question that demands to be answered.

I had sent him away; had turned my back on the one thing in this world that I knew and understood. My sole skill was the giving of pleasure – but I had sent Richard upstairs alone. And what was left for me now? I had been built to be a courtesan. Now, it seemed, I was a courtesan no longer. What could I do? Who could I be?

Nothing. No-one. The air around me seemed to tighten like a giant hand, until I almost felt my cogs buckle under the pressure of it.

'Help me,' I whispered to the empty room. 'Help me. Please.'

The door swung open.

'Richard, where's the – oh.' Lechasseur stood there in his shirt sleeves, looking faintly annoyed. 'I thought Richard was in here.'

'He – went upstairs.'

'Oh well, never mind.' He turned to go.

'Honoré, wait!'

He paused with his hand on the door-handle, and looked back at me.

I would rather a thousand times that it had been Emily who had come in, and not him. Emily I liked, trusted, knew as a friend; but this man hid himself behind a blank expression and a polite smile, and I had no idea what lay behind that wall. Yet help I had to have, or I felt as though I should die; so I forced myself to speak.

'I am afraid,' I said softly. 'I do not know what to do.'

'What do you mean, afraid?'

I struggled to find the right words. 'I – feel as though my life, everything I thought was my life, has been ripped away from me, and I am standing alone before a terrible light. I feel as though my world is in ruins about me.'

He shrugged. 'Then build yourself a new world. Find someone else to be.'

'You make it sound so simple,' I said bitterly, thinking he was setting my suffering lightly aside.

Lechasseur came a few paces into the room, and to my surprise I saw compassion in his face. 'No, it's not simple. It's not easy, either.'

'You – speak as one who knows,' I said slowly.

'Yeah, I know.' He turned to leave, but I sprang forward, clutching at his arm.

'Then tell me! In God's name, tell me! I am lost and most alone – tell me what I must do!'

Gently he set me aside. 'It's not something I usually talk about.'

'This is not usually – this is *now*!'

'Well, it's not something I *want* to talk about.' Again he made to leave. I flung myself in front of him, and set my back against the door.

'You must tell me, you must! You shall not leave this room until you tell me!' I was wild, half-crazed, knowing only that I was drowning, and reaching blindly for a floating spar. 'Tell me!' I demanded. '*Tell me!*'

And then, at last, he spoke. His voice was low, but I have never heard any shout or cry that could have won my attention so wholly as those quiet tones did. 'When the world is pulled out from under you – when it feels like you'll never get it back – you can start to feel like you're lost. You can start to give up, just because it's so much easier. They tell you you won't walk again, and maybe it would be simpler not to. To lie back and let people bring you things. But you don't. You learn to walk, you make a life for yourself, you find a way to carry on. That's what you do.

Maybe it gets easier as it goes on. Maybe you even enjoy it, in a cold kind of way. But nothing really *touches* you. Not until – '

He stopped. 'Until?' I prompted gently.

'Something changes,' he said quietly, 'There's a shift. It all starts to feel . . . right. As though everything that was broken is knitting itself together again. Slowly, maybe, but it's happening. But then – sweet *Jesus*!' The cry rang in the silent room. 'I didn't know what time was any more, or even what the world was, or whether it was the whole universe that was going insane or just me; and then I *knew* it was just me, and that was worse than ever . . . '

He was no longer speaking to me. His eyes were focused on something very far away, and the look on his face made my own agony seem suddenly small and insignificant. When Emily had opened her heart to me, it had been the gentle unfolding of a flower. But the confiding of Honoré Lechasseur was a sword-blade flashing free. It stabbed me through to my core.

A wave of remorse swamped me. I had been treating Lechasseur in the same way that others had treated me – as a thing to be made use of, not as a person at all. Indeed, when had I *ever* seen him as a person. He had been to me a hero, a rescuer – and is a hero allowed a personality? Fear and doubt are not permitted him, hesitation would endanger the already perilous enterprise. A hero must never flinch. Never falter.

Never be human.

'Honoré, I am sorry,' I said, stepping away from the door. 'I did not mean to hurt you. I – I did not even think you *could* be hurt. Forgive me.'

His eyes refocused, and he smiled at me. 'Well, of course I can. I'm only human, you know.'

I glanced aside. 'While I – am somewhat less than that.'

About to leave the door, Lechasseur paused with his hand on the door-knob. 'Oh, I'm not so sure about that,' he said, gently.

Before I could respond, he had gone.

I stood alone in the library. The night stretched empty ahead of me, as so many other nights had before. Idly I took up the book that still lay on the small table, and, sinking into a well-stuffed leather chair, opened it at random.

The first object of laudable ambition is to obtain a character as a human being . . . The words caught my eye, arresting me.

A character as a human being. I knew that I was a woman; a clockwork woman, formed to be docile, obedient, and pliable – a model of feminine perfection. But now I was no longer docile, had ceased to be pliable, and had left obedience far behind. *Find someone else to be* . . . A human being? Could I even aspire to that?

I turned to the first page, and began to read in earnest.

Independence I have long considered as the grand blessing of life, the basis of every virtue; and independence I will ever secure by contracting my wants, though I were to live on a barren heath. Independence! There was a fine, ringing sound to that word. I spoke it softly aloud to myself, and found that I liked the way it felt in my mouth. Turning the pages, I read on.

The mind must be strong that resolutely forms its own principles; for a kind of intellectual cowardice prevails which makes many men shrink from the task, or only do it by halves. Here, for the first time, I hesitated. I had, I realised, hoped that the book that lay open on my lap might act as a guide, a set of instructions on how to live my new life. That, in short, it would give me a series of second-hand principles, which I could imbibe without the trouble of too much mental exertion. But now . . . *The mind must be strong that resolutely forms its own principles.* Did I have that kind of strength? For the first time, I perceived that independence might be a quality of the mind, as well as of the body. More slowly now, I read on.

If it be allowed that women were destined by Providence to acquire human virtues, and, by the exercise of their understandings, that stability of character which is the firmest ground to rest our future hopes upon . . . This was stirring – this was vibrant! *Human virtues* – that gave me hope, and I bent closer to the page. But then, in solemn counterpoint, the words *exercise of their understandings* made me recoil a little in apprehension. And here, again, as I turned the page, I found the theme rung in. *Every being may become virtuous by the exercise of its own reason* . . . *It is a farce to call any being virtuous whose virtues do not result from the exercise of its own reason.* More and more, it was becoming clear to me that this was no simple instruction book that might lead me to easy paths. Again and again I was brought back to face that which I feared – for fear it I did. I did not want to have to venture unguided on the trackless ways of Reason, of Understanding, where I had never been before. I was not built to think for myself. It was not part of my design.

But still I read on.

Strengthen the female mind by enlarging it, and there will be an end to blind obedience; but as blind obedience is ever sought for by power, tyrants and sensualists are in the right when they endeavour to keep women in the dark, because the former only want slaves, and the latter a plaything. Now, with those words, a light seemed to glow far off. Not strong enough to make clear the path at my feet, but enough to make me wish to step forward, risky though it might be. For if thinking for myself might make me free forever of men like Sir Edward, of men such as Sir Richard – if finding the strength to reason independently would free me from both the tyrant and the sensualist – then the journey was worth it, whatever pitfalls I might encounter along the way.

It is time to effect a revolution in female manners – time to restore to them their lost dignity – and make them, as a part of the human species, labour by reforming themselves to reform the world. A new light shone for me. Though the path was dark still, the destination grew ever brighter. For if it was not only I who could be aided and transformed by this journey – if my own change could be made a small cog in the change and improvement of the whole world – then surely it was not only cowardly to turn aside. It was wrong.

Can she rest supinely dependent on man for reason, when she ought to mount with him the arduous steeps of knowledge? Again I found myself stirred by her words, and turned the pages with increasing fervour.

If wisdom be desirable on its own account, if virtue, to deserve the name, must be founded on knowledge, let us endeavour to strengthen our minds by reflection till our heads become a balance for our hearts; let us not confine all our thoughts to the petty occurrences of the day, or our knowledge to an acquaintance with our lovers' or our husbands' hearts, but let the practice of every duty be subordinate to the grand one of improving our minds . . . I trembled; but I acquiesced. And when I read the words, *they alone are subject to blind authority who have no reliance on their own strength,* I vowed to myself that I would learn such reliance, though it might take me a century or more.

And soon, a picture of this tired old world – not as it *is*, but as it *could be*, began to be sketched out before me. *Women ought to have represen-*

tatives, instead of being arbitrarily governed without having any share allowed them in the deliberations of government ... Women might certainly study the politics, and settle their benevolence on the broadest bases ... Business of various kinds, they might likewise pursue ... they must have a civil existence in the State, married or single ... Tyrants would have cause to tremble if reason were to become a role of duty in any of the relations of life, for the light might spread till perfect day appeared ... Reason and experience convince me that the only method of leading women to fulfil their ... duties is to free them from all restraint by allowing them to participate in the inherent rights of mankind ... I drew it all in eagerly, almost dazzled by the glorious depiction. Surely this was worth fighting for, whatever might be the difficulties along the way! And when I reached the triumphant cry, *The most salutary effects tending to improve mankind might be expected from a REVOLUTION in female manners,* I found myself trembling a little – not from fear this time, but from excitement.

It was at that moment that I heard the sound of a loud cry from upstairs. Starting to my feet, I was out of the library and mounting the stairs almost before I thought. The only two people in the world I cared for lay asleep up there.

As I reached the head of the stairs, there was a sudden, thunderous report. It came from a door to my left, which I wrenched open in a frenzy of terror.

On the four-poster bed that stood in the middle of the room, Sir Richard lay. Or at least, his head lay there, as did his legs, his forearms, and much of the lower part of his torso. The rest had been blasted into a red mist that was spattered liberally about the sheets and bed-hangings.

He had threatened me, sought to use me, shown no regard for my feelings. He had also helped to rescue Emily and me from a life of subjugation. He had fallen in with Lechasseur's plans for our rescue, and without him those plans would never have come to fruition. Perhaps part of his motivation had been to get a pretty girl into his debt and his power, but part of it at least must have been simple human feeling, kindness, compassion, call it what you will. I owed him a great deal. And he had been a human being, a man who lived and loved, laughed and fought. He had planned for his future, had enjoyed the life he lived. Now he was a smeared, bloody thing that made me give an involuntary cry of disgust to see it.

A movement by the window arrested my attention. I turned, and saw –
Sir Edward.

I believe we must have remained standing in shock, staring at each
other, for at least five seconds. I could not have moved in those seconds,
even if I had tried to. This was Sir Edward, my creator, my owner, the
man who had once been all in all to me. Until a few days ago, my only
wish, my only desire, had been to please him. Now that life seemed
divided from me by a great gulf, as though it had been a hundred years
ago, or a dream. And yet he was here, he stood before me, and, against
my will, I found myself drawn to him, yearning towards him. If he had
stood there for even a moment longer, I truly believe I would have run
into his arms. But even as the impulse formed in my mind, a spasm of
some unrecognisable emotion crossed Sir Edward's face, twisting it until
it seemed more animal than human; and he turned from me towards
the window. In a moment, he was gone, leaving only the curtains swaying
a little in the night breeze.

I did not go in pursuit. I might have done. I might even have caught
him, and thus saved myself and my friends many troubles that afterwards
befell. But I was too bewildered, too dumbfounded by what had just
occurred, to do anything but stand and gape.

I heard the sound of someone crashing through the undergrowth of
Richard's garden; then the noise faded away, and I knew that Sir Edward
had gone. As though his absence released the power of thought and
action in me, I found I could move again. Running to the window, I saw
no sign of him; and I turned back into the room, to where the thing lay
smeared and bloody on the bed.

You will think me callous, but I barely glanced at it, so caught up was I
in my own turmoil. I had thought – had begun to think – that I might be
free at last, free of the life Sir Edward had designed me for. Yet that one
brief sight of him had shown me how far that was from being true. All my
joy in the new world that Wollstonecraft had shown me, all my half-
formed, tentative hopes, had been swept away by that one sight of Sir
Edward. And I knew, as though I had seen it written on tablets of stone by
the hand of God, that I could not now turn away. I could not ignore this
thing that had happened, and go forth, hoping to make a life for myself.

No, I could not go forth. Instead, I would have to go back. I would
have to see Sir Edward, one last time. Whether I would kill him, submit

to him, ask him to explain, spit in his face or kneel at his feet, I did not know. I did not even truly know why it was that I had to return. I knew only that return I must, in response to a prompting that went deeper than logic or reason.

Barely had I formed this conclusion when I heard footsteps coming along the corridor. So bound up was I with my own concerns, it took me a moment to struggle free of them. By the time I did, it was too late.

'Stop!' I cried. 'Go back – do not look –' But they had already entered the chamber.

Emily gave a small cry of horror, and put up her hands before her face. Lechasseur only stared grimly, his face drained of blood until his skin was an unhealthy shade of grey.

'I am sorry,' I said weakly, 'I tried to warn you.' But I knew that I had not tried hard enough.

'Who did it?' Lechasseur asked briefly.

'It was Sir Edward. I saw him. He carried a gun of his own design.'

'He designed a gun that could do *that*?' Emily asked in a whisper.

'He did. And worse.' I hesitated, but could not long hold myself back from speaking. 'I must go back. I have to –' I faltered and stopped.

Emily turned towards me, concern in her eyes. 'Dove? You have to . . . what?'

'I do not know,' I said, honestly. 'It is only that – that when I saw him, I realised there was unfinished business between us. What it is, I do not yet know. But I must go back.'

'We're coming too,' said Lechasseur, in a tone that brooked no argument.

I tried to protest, all the same. 'No, it is my fight – '

'We're coming,' Emily repeated. 'Dove, there's something we need to do here. Something important. Until it's done, we've got to stick close to you.'

I looked from one to the other, bewildered. 'What is this thing?'

'We don't know,' Lechasseur answered cryptically. 'But we'll know when we've done it.'

And though I questioned them, neither one would say any more.

We took money from Richard's bureau (Emily protested, but Lechasseur ignored her), and took a post-chaise up to Sir Edward's estate. I cannot say what the others thought of during the drive; there was little conversation, and that little consisted mostly of the kind of inconsequential observations on the weather and the state of the roads that we might have made had we been strangers who had happened to find themselves travelling together. I think we were all stunned by what had just happened. I know I was.

As the carriage jolted its way along the roads, I tried to make sense of the tumbling whirl of emotions that the killing of Sir Richard had flung me into. There was the horror of seeing a dead man, for the first time ever in my life; and so dreadfully, so violently dead! I shuddered to think of it. I had seen dismantled robots in Sir Edward's workshop, but never a human being dead.

Then there was a stubborn sensation of guilt, that I could not push away. I had been built to serve Sir Edward, and I had gone against that. At first, my rebellion had almost destroyed me (and even yet I flinched from the memory of Sir Edward lying unconscious at my feet), but, like all other things, it had become easier with usage. Usage, and separation; for Sir Edward had been so far away, it had been a relatively simple matter to banish the thought of him from my mind. But now . . . now, I had seen him again, had felt that instinctive urge, implanted in my deepest programming, to go to him and serve him once more. And though I had not done so, that moment had awakened all the servile feelings in me again. I ought to have stayed, I ought to have stayed – the thought hammered insistently in my brain, and refused to be set aside. How could I have left him so? How cruel of me it had been!

I shook my head violently, pushing such thoughts from me. I would not allow myself to feel remorse – I had had a right to my freedom! It was Sir Edward who ought to be suffering from guilt, for having created such a being as myself and bound her to him, body and soul . . . Soul? Did I even possess such a thing?

But – my mind returned to an earlier conundrum, worrying it like a dog with a bone – why had he come to London? Had it been to search for me? But then, why should he have flown as soon as he had found me? After puzzling on this for a while, I cast it aside. We were now returning to the place where the answers might be found; a place I feared to go, even as another part of my being yearned for it beyond all expression. Sir Edward's house. My birthplace. My home.

'We're here,' Lechasseur said abruptly. I looked up in surprise. We had indeed arrived at the turnstile that was as near as this coach would go to our destination. The coach drew to a stop, and we got out. Now we would have to take the footpath across the fields and past the village to Sir Edward's house. I shivered, then clenched my fists. I had said I would do this, and I would do it.

We set off along the path. Soon, the village came into view. The footpath wound close to it, we would almost brush against it as we passed. As we drew closer, I began to notice something rather strange. There were no children running and playing in the fields; more disturbingly, there were no labourers at work in them. I knew little about the seasons for farming; but surely there should have been some people out working? Then, as we approached close enough to the village to hear sounds wafted on the wind, things became even stranger. For the only sound we heard was that of one man, shouting. Not in fear, or pain, or rage; it sounded as though he was haranguing someone, in a long, loud, ferocious speech.

Lechasseur, Emily and I glanced at one another. The next turn of the path would take us away from the village. I could tell from the look on Emily's face that she wanted to keep walking, but she said nothing.

'Let's go closer,' said Lechasseur. 'I want to hear what they're saying.'

Now Emily broke her silence. 'Couldn't we just go straight on? What's the point in getting mixed up in trouble?'

'I want to hear what they're saying,' Lechasseur repeated stubbornly.

Emily glanced at me to see if I would offer her support, but I gave none. I was torn; I wanted to stop and find out what was happening, but I also wanted to hurry back to Sir Edward's house. But then, I feared that house as much as I desired it . . . I made no resistance when Lechasseur turned and led the way towards the village. Emily, sighing a little under her breath, followed him as well.

As we rounded the corner into the village square, we saw a strange sight. All the villagers were clustered around one man, who stood on what seemed to be an improvised plinth, and spat out his words with angry gestures.

'And I say they *can't* be exorcised! Curate went to exorcise 'em – where's curate now? I'll *tell* you where. Curate's been caught by 'em, that's what!'

We edged closer. The audience were so absorbed in the man's speech that they didn't even notice us, and we managed to creep up until we were standing on the outskirts of the crowd.

'And *I* say,' the man continued, 'I say witches called 'em! Find the witch, you find the cause! Find the cause' – he paused, and his face twisted into an ugly expression of malice –'and yer can *destroy* the cause. Find the witches that called them . . . things, and kill 'em! That'll send them hell-hounds back where they came from.'

Emily plucked at Lechasseur's sleeve. 'I don't like this,' she whispered urgently. 'We should go.' But he shook her off impatiently, and turned back to the speaker.

The audience had begun to mutter among themselves, speculating about the possible identity of the witch. 'It couldn't be anyone from the village,' a woman called out finally. 'I won't believe it could have been any of us!'

The man on the plinth shook his head. 'No. It couldn't be any of us. We've all lost a brother or a wife or' – he shuddered, passing his hand across his face – 'or a child. It couldn't be any of us.'

'Then *who*?' shrilled a voice.

Seemingly at a loss for the first time, the man gazed around the audience. And saw the three of us.

His eye lit with sudden hate. 'It was *them*!' he cried, pointing at us with a finger that trembled. 'Don't you remember how, just before the hounds started their attacks, a harlot and a Blackamoor stayed at our little inn? Our quiet inn, that'd never seen anything such as that before. And the harlot seduced the curate while the Blackamoor watched! It was part of the spell! Look at them, back to gloat at us in our distress! They've brought their other harlot – three's a coven, everyone knows that! And all Blackamoors worship demons!' He was shouting now, foam flecking his chin, and dozens of hard, eager hands were reaching out to take hold of us. Before we could even think of running, we were seized and dragged down the street, pulled this way and that by the furious villagers.

'Take them to the Inn's cellar!' shouted the original speech-maker, above the tumult. 'Lock them in! Make the sign of the cross on the door to make sure they can't get out! Then bring all the firewood you can find. We've got to burn out the evil!'

We were tumbled into blackness, and the door slammed upon us. Then it was almost pitch-dark in the cellar where we were confined, with only a very little light seeping under the cellar door.

There was a long silence. Finally, Emily spoke. 'Maybe it wasn't such a good idea to go into the village after all.'

Lechasseur sighed a long sigh. 'Look,' he said quietly, 'if you want me to say that I'm really sorry, that you were right and I was wrong, then I will. But that won't get us out of this, will it?'

'No,' Emily replied, 'it won't.' There was silence for a moment, then Lechasseur added: 'I just wish I knew what that guy was talking about.'

'I – think I know,' I said, and heard the faint rustle of his clothing as he shifted round to look at me.

'Well?'

'He was talking about Sir Edward's attack dogs.' I paused, and took a deep breath. 'Do you remember how he said that the hell-hounds appeared just after we arrived?'

'Of course!' Lechasseur's voice was excited, almost pleased. 'And we already know that Sir Edward came down to London to look for you – he must have left the gates of his estate open, and the dogs must have escaped!'

I nodded. A useless gesture, since no-one could see it in the dark. I shared none of Lechasseur's pleasure – my thoughts were spinning inexorably around the fact that, if I had never left, Sir Edward would never have gone to London to find me, he would not have left the gates open, and none of the villagers would have died. How could my own freedom possibly be worth the deaths of all those innocent people?

Lechasseur's voice broke into my uncomfortable musings. 'It's time we got out of here,' he said briskly.

'That may be easier said than done,' replied Emily, a note a fear now creeping into her voice.

'Wait a minute . . . ' Quietly, Lechasseur crept over to the door. After a moment, he said, softly, 'I can't hear anything. I think they've all gone off to build a bonfire. Quick, search around, both of you, we need to find a nail or something.'

We all groped around on the floor for long moments. Finally, Emily gave a triumphant hiss. 'Here's one!'

'Give it here.' Lechasseur fumbled for it in the dark, examined it for a moment, then grunted. 'It'll have to do. Now, be quiet for a bit. I'm going to have to concentrate.'

We sat in silence while he worked away at the lock, swearing softly whenever the nail slipped. Finally, there was a small click, and the door swung open, allowing light to flood in.

We crept out of the cellar. There was a series of three rough steps that led from the cellar door to the street level, and the three of us crouched at the bottom of them, peering over the lip. We were on a street that led directly to the main square, and could clearly see the villagers piling up wood to make a pyre. More to the point, once we moved from our impromptu hiding place, they would be able to see us, if they happened to glance up from their work.

'What shall we do?' I asked.

'Run,' Lechasseur answered. 'It's the only way. But try to run quietly.'

Emily looked at him. 'Run *quietly*?'

'Shh. Come on.'

We pelted down the street, I with my skirts gathered in both hands to keep me from tripping. We might even have made it, if one of the enthusiastic bonfire builders hadn't chosen that moment to straighten up from his work.

'Look! The witches are getting away!'

We put on an extra spurt of speed; but Emily, smallest and slightest of us three, now began to gasp and fall behind. With a glance at each other, Lechasseur and I caught her by the arms and dragged her onwards. But now the burden slowed us. We were on the very outskirts of the village when the crowd caught us up.

Lechasseur, letting go of Emily's arm, turned at bay, swinging round into a punch that lifted the foremost of our pursuers off his feet, sending him flying back into his fellows. That made them pause for a moment, and Lechasseur snapped, 'Run!' over his shoulder at us.

'Not without you!' Emily said fiercely; and, pulling free from my grip, she moved to stand beside him. He pushed her back towards me.

'Dove, get her out of here!'

Emily looked up at me. 'Dove, no! We can't leave him to be burned!'

I looked at Emily, at Lechasseur. Then I looked at the villagers, who were standing bewildered, watching us quarrel. This wasn't their idea of what witches should be like. They were confused, off balance. We should be using that. But how? I had no idea. Frantically, I caught Lechasseur's eye, and nodded fractionally towards the milling villagers. He looked at me, then at them. I saw a plan forming in his eyes.

The moment before the mob might have overcome their incomprehension and rushed us anyway, Lechasseur took a sudden step towards them, startling them so that they surged back from him in a body.

'Did you think your puny cross could keep me in?' he cried, his voice a menacing rasp. 'Well, it couldn't! I can fly through windows, I can seep through doors. Leave us be, or I will call down the hell-hounds to tear your flesh from your bones!'

For a moment, the mob stood silent. Then they broke and ran, dashing down the street. Lechasseur grabbed Emily and me by the arms. 'Come on,' he said urgently, 'In a moment or so they'll come to their senses and wonder why we didn't just call the hounds when they went to lock us up. Let's get out of here!'

We ran away from the village, and did not look back.

Finally, we paused, and flung ourselves on the ground to rest.

'Where are we now?' Emily panted. 'I wasn't keeping track.'

I sat up and looked around. I remembered some of this landscape from Lechasseur's and my earlier tramp across it to reach the village, the night I ran away. 'I believe Sir Edward's house is over in that direction,' I said, pointing.

Lechasseur began to get to his feet. 'Well, we'd better get going then.'

At that moment, we heard a howl, faint and far-off in the distance. The three of us looked at each other, the same terrible realisation striking all of us simultaneously.

'The attack dogs!' we said in unison.

The howl came again, still far-off but closer than before.

'It's between us and the house,' Lechasseur commented grimly.

'They,' I corrected him.

He looked at me. 'They?'

'The dogs always hunt in packs,' I explained. 'There is bound to be more than one of them.'

He slapped his forehead with his palm. 'Oh, great.'

Emily got to her feet. 'We should go,' she said nervously, 'We should run.'

I rose too. 'We should go, yes; but not start running just yet. It may be that they do not even know we are out here. We should walk away from the direction of the sound; and if we can find a place to hide, we should do so.'

'You're forgetting,' Lechasseur pointed out, rising in his turn. 'They'd be able to sniff us out. Just because you don't leave a scent trail, that doesn't mean we don't.'

He was right, I had forgotten. I nodded silently, and we set off, walking away from the sound of the howls. But they didn't diminish in the distance. Every time we heard them, they seemed to be closer. We glanced at each other; and, by mutual, unspoken consent, began to run.

But the howls of the dogs grew closer and closer still, and now I could tell that there was quite a large pack pursuing us. Lechasseur seemed to have come to the same conclusion, for he suddenly came to a halt and gasped, 'We should split up. Emily, go that way, Dove, go the other way. I'll go this way. If we can confuse them, divide the pack, we stand a better chance of getting away.'

Emily and I glanced at each other. We knew that he was in the right of it. Wasting no breath on discussing it, I silently turned and begun running in the direction he had indicated. Glancing back briefly, I saw Emily and Lechasseur clasp hands for a moment in a kind of good-bye, then turn and start running in different directions. Then I looked to my own flight, and settled into my own pace.

There came a point when the sounds behind me began to grow fainter, and I felt a huge, shameful wave of relief. I didn't leave a scent trail – there was no way for the dogs to follow me. They had gone after Emily and Lechasseur. I was safe. I still ran on, though – ran blindly, unthinkingly, desperate to put as much distance between me and the dogs as possible. And that was my downfall; for I was so intent on running, simply running, that I didn't even notice when the ground beneath my feet began to slope upwards. I just ran on, up the hill, up and further up, until, pausing for a rest, I happened to glance behind me, and realised I was on quite an eminence.

From here, I could see Emily and Lechasseur, tiny doll-like figures against the muddy green background of the moors, and the glint of the two packs of dogs that separately pursued them, steadily gaining. I stood a long moment, wringing my hands in a positive agony of impotence. So caught up was I in the drama unfolding below me, I remained quite unaware of my own danger. Until one of the dogs, pausing and casting around for the scent trail, raised its head. And saw me.

I had forgotten – had simply not thought – that if I could see the dogs, they could certainly see me. The one that had turned its head in my direction gave a long, low howl, and its pack-fellows all looked up as one. There was a long moment of stillness, and then, as though by common consent, half the pack (it was the one pursuing Emily, I noted automatically) split off, heading for the place where I stood.

That jolted me out of my horrified rigidity. I turned, and ran up the hill once more.

But now the howls from behind me no longer faded into the distance. Instead, they grew closer; closer; closer still. Now I could feel my gears groaning and juddering under the strain, but still the dogs came mercilessly on.

Raising my eyes from the track for a moment, I saw that I was heading towards a rocky escarpment, and moaned under my breath. In this state, I would have trouble climbing rocks, while the dogs, tireless as they were, would have no such difficulty. But it was too late to try to detour around it, so I flung myself at the rocks and began to climb. After a short time – too short! – I looked down and saw the dogs below me, transforming to their humanoid shapes, rising to their hind legs and extending their claws for the climb. They came up preternaturally quickly, moving with twice the speed I could coax out of my own, tired body. Desperately, hopelessly, I scrambled on. Now the rocks were levelling out, but still I had to haul myself past great teeth and claws of stone, thrust up in my way as though the landscape itself were a huge stone dog, and wished to aid its fellows.

At last I tripped, and fell full-length. The dogs were close behind me; I could hear the scraping of their claws against the rocks. I knew, deep in the core of me, that I would never be able to escape them. But I could meet my death standing, at least. I pushed myself half-upright with my hands –

And saw, directly in front of me, a small niche in the rocks. Not large enough to be dignified with the name of 'cave', it was nevertheless wide enough to admit a slim body. A body such as mine. In a moment, I was at the lip, and dragging myself inside. Thanks be to God! It was deep enough to hide me. But only just. If one of the dogs should glance inside, it would be all up with me. I heard the pack come baying over the rocks, and held myself still.

They passed me by.

I lay limp in the rock cleft, barely able to comprehend my own reprieve. They had passed. I was safe. The dogs possessed limited, basic instincts. They would hunt down and kill any living thing they saw, heard or smelled; but they did not have the wit to look back and work out that I would be hiding in the rocks. Once they realised they had lost my trail, they would howl in frustration before finding someone else to chase.

Someone else . . . With a jolt, I remembered that my friends were still in danger. No, not merely in danger; almost certainly doomed. Unlike me, they could not simply hide. As Lechasseur had pointed out, the dogs would be able to follow their scents. But what could I do? What on earth could I –

Then I realised what I could do; and the knowledge was like ice in my mind. I could return to Sir Edward's house. I could ask the housekeeper to restrain the dogs. They were answerable to it – it could instruct them at its will. It might well be that I, as Sir Edward's toy, had enough authority to order it to obey me. It was all eminently logical. And yet I lay still in the crevice, and did not move.

I do not want to go to Sir Edward's house. I had come all this way to do just that, and now it was all in vain. I could not, would not return. I would creep away softly, evading the dogs, I –

I, said a small voice in my mind. *I, I, I. Do you say nothing else? Do you care for nothing else? Your friends are at risk of death because they were loyal to you. And you, you would abandon them – for what? Because you seem to think your own feelings, your own sensibility, is more important than two human lives. Truly are you Sir Edward's creation.*

I covered my ears, but the voice was inside me. It was part of me, a part I had never known of before. And what was more, it spoke the truth. I had been selfish, had put myself before my friends. I was disgusted with myself, I –

No, said the voice. *No more I. There is no time for you to wallow in remorse. Your friends are in danger. Go now.*

I slipped out of the crevice, and set off towards Sir Edward's house.

I hauled myself in over the windowsill, and dropped quietly to the carpet inside. Looking around, I saw that I was standing in a long corridor. I recognised the place at once. The kitchens were in *that* direction, I recalled, and the housekeeper's room was *that* way. So the nearest speaking-tube was – just around the corner. I tiptoed along the carpet, as softly as I could, until I stood directly below it. Now, of course, I would have to speak, and simply hope that Sir Edward was in some other part of the house, where he would not be able to hear me.

'Housekeeper!'

There was no reply.

'Housekeeper!' I called again, a little louder this time.

'Yes?' came the calm, familiar tones I remembered so well.

'Housekeeper, do you know me?'

'I know you. You are Sir Edward's toy.'

I hesitated; but this was no time to quibble over designations. 'That is right. I am. And I want you to call off the attack dogs.'

'You have no right to instruct me,' the housekeeper informed me politely. 'Only Sir Edward may instruct me.'

I paused. I knew that there was no time for delay, that what I had come to do was urgent; but the housekeeper's words had stirred me to intense curiosity. As quickly as I could, I asked, 'Where *is* Sir Edward?'

'He is in his room.'

'His *room*? But it is the middle of the day! What is he doing there?'

'I do not know.'

My curiosity was unsatisfied, but I could delay longer. Every moment might bring the death of one of my friends. 'Housekeeper, you must call off the dogs!'

'Sir Edward has given me no orders to,' it answered, unmoved.

I sank back against the wall, feeling my old trembling begin again. For it was clear to me that no pleading would move the housekeeper, no curses affect it. I had hoped that my status as the favoured toy might have given me sufficient authority to command it, but now this hope was starkly torn away, and I was left quite alone and naked. There was no Lechasseur to rescue me, no Emily to advise me. My friends were not able to come to my aid; instead, I must come to theirs. And this was not a situation in which the tricks of seduction or the skills of a courtesan would be of any use to me at all. The housekeeper could not be wiled, could not be weakened.

And now the task to which I had vowed myself in the still quiet of the early morning took hold of me with devastating force. For now I must think alone, must act alone, or else my friends would die. And yet I stood helpless, paralysed, shaking hard; for now the necessity was upon me, I found I could not do it.

'I was not built for this!' I moaned aloud, pressing my hands to my temples. 'I was not made for it! Oh, God have mercy on me, I *cannot* think!'

The mind must be strong that resolutely forms its own principles; for a kind of intellectual cowardice prevails which makes many men shrink from the task.

'It is not cowardice!' I cried aloud, heedless now of who might hear me. 'I tell you I cannot!'

Every being may become virtuous by the exercise of its own reason.

'But I *have* no reason! I was not built with reason – Sir Edward did not build me so! Oh God help me, God help me, *I am still his toy!*'

They alone are subject to blind authority who have no reliance on their own strength. They are free – who will be free!

'They are free . . . who will be free . . . ' I said softly, and pushed myself slowly upright, away from the wall.

The blank, black mouthpiece of the housekeeper thrust from the wall above me. I turned my head to look up at it, and clenched my fists hard.

'Housekeeper!'

'Yes?'

'Do you know that the dogs have been killing the children from the village?'

'That is not my concern,' it answered, unmoved.

'But it is!'

'Why?'

Yes, why? Why should the housekeeper, which cared about none but Sir Edward, be disturbed at the deaths of children? How could I *make* it disturbed?

And even as I asked myself the question, the beginnings of an answer crept through my mind.

'Housekeeper, the villagers are angry – they want revenge for the deaths of their children.'

'That is not my concern.'

'But what if they decide to take revenge on Sir Edward?'

'They would not dare.' Was there the faintest hint of hesitation in the housekeeper's voice, or was it only my desperate hope deceiving me?

'They dare a great deal,' I cried, 'They have dared to lock up me and my friends with the intention of killing us! And now we have escaped, they have no-one on whom to vent their anger. Their rage will turn against Sir Edward, they will come against him with pitchforks, and knives, and fire! They will come to burn him out – they will come to kill him!'

'You are lying.' Now I was sure I had heard a hesitation, a brief faltering in the smooth, emotionless voice.

'I am made by Sir Edward. Do you believe that he could create an imperfect thing? A thing that did wrong?'

'No.'

'And is not lying wrong?'

'Yes.'

I felt a fierce exultation. Now it was trapped! By its own logic, its own devotion to Sir Edward, I had trapped it. Now I must tighten the noose. 'They will come to kill him, and he has no protection! You must call off the dogs – you must set them in a phalanx at the gate. It is the only way to save him!'

'I have no orders!' cried the housekeeper; and for the first time in my existence, I heard dismay in that passionless voice.

'If you keep to your orders, Sir Edward will die. But call off the dogs, and you save him!'

'I must obey Sir Edward . . . ' groaned the machine, in a voice like rending metal.

'Obey him or save him – you cannot do both. The villagers will come – they are coming now! They are almost at the gates! You must decide quickly!'

'I cannot . . . '

'Obey him or save him!'

'No . . . '

'*Choose!*'

The housekeeper gave one last, terrible cry; then silence fell. I stood quite still, in a great terror, for a reason that I could not understand. In another moment, I had it; the sound of the housekeeper was gone. All my days, I had heard that soft, omnipresent hum, pervading all the corridors of the house so that I had come to associate it with the house itself, and had not been consciously aware of it. Until it ceased. Now the silence seemed to ring dreadfully in my ears; and, feeling close to panic,

I gathered up my skirts in my hands, and ran towards the housekeeper's room.

I stood in the doorway. The great, grey block of the housekeeper squatted still in the centre of the room. But the dull red glow of the pilot light was extinguished; and I knew, with an unexpected pang, that my aim was achieved. The housekeeper, asked to make a decision on its own, had broken down under the pressure of it. Without it, the dogs would be nothing but inert lumps of metal. I had succeeded; and had destroyed what had been, in its emotionless way, the only mother I had ever known. I put my hand gently on one of the pipes that ran from the dead housekeeper, and drew my fingers along it for a moment.

'You could have tried to think a little,' I murmured. 'It is – not so very hard, when once you begin.'

There was an inarticulate cry behind me. I whirled, ready to fight or flee. Sir Edward stood there, his arms extended; but, I realised after a moment of utter panic, not to grasp or attack me. His hands were held out in a gesture of welcome; and there were tears in his eyes.

'You came back,' he whispered. 'Oh, my darling, you came back.'

I made him no reply, only stood stock-still and stared at him. He was not as I had known him, not the well-clad, urbane man whom I had looked up to without question as master and creator. His clothes were filthy, his face haggard and pale, his frame wasted. Had he been so when I had seen him in London? I could not recall. I had seen him only for a brief moment, and the shock of recognition had driven all things else from my mind. But now, as he stood before me, I looked, and I saw.

'Dear God, Sir Edward,' I cried, in genuine dismay. 'You are changed – you are greatly changed! Who has done this to you?'

He gazed at me, mournfully. 'You did, my angel,' he said, softly. 'When you struck me – and I woke to find you gone – I couldn't stand it, I thought I should go mad. I found out from the villagers where you'd gone, I rode down on the unicorn, I tried to trace you. God! That city – ' He shuddered and drew his hand across his eyes. 'But I found you, I found you – oh my dearest, I would have taken you away from that terrible brothel, would have *bought* you back if there had been no other way! Why didn't you wait? Why did you go off with them?'

'Wait – ?' I shook my head, bewildered. 'You saw that? How?'

'I was hiding on the other side of the street,' he answered simply. 'I thought, if I spied the place out for a night, I would be better able to lay plans to rescue you.'

'Oh, of course,' I murmured, my mind running on what he must have endured. He would have had to question rough, churlish men and women who would have been more likely to spit at him than return a civil answer; would probably have had to lodge in some ill-run boarding house – and how in God's name had he managed to conceal a unicorn, of all things, in the streets of such a bustling metropolis as London? But he had begun to speak again, and I returned my attention to his tale.

'I had to do it, I had to!' he said now, pleading almost. 'When I knew that he must have won you away from me, I had to do what I did! But when you came into the room and cried out like that – and I knew you must have loved him – I thought, she'll never forgive me for this, never come back to me now – I couldn't stand it – I couldn't . . . The unicorn broke down at the gates of the estate. I had to walk back to the house – I shut myself in my room, I haven't eaten – I've barely slept! I thought you'd never come back to me – but you have! Oh, God bless you for it!'

He made as though to clasp me; but I was faster than he, and stepped back, out of his reach. His speech had made me recall what the pathos of his appearance had temporarily displaced from my memory; that this man was a murderer. Indeed, a murderer many times over; for, by omitting to call off the dogs, he had allowed I knew not how many of the villagers to die most cruelly.

'Sir Edward,' I asked, still standing off from him, 'why did you let the dogs run free? You must have known they would do much harm.'

He looked at me in amazement, as though I had asked him something that had neither relevance nor importance. 'Why, it was when I came back from London, my dear. I left the gate open when I entered, for I was so dispirited that I could not summon the energy to shut it, or even to care whether it was open or shut. But I shall never be so sad again, now you are come back – ' Again he made to seize me; again I eluded him.

'But the dogs are built to kill!' I cried. 'Did you not think of the deaths you would cause?'

'I told you, beloved, I cared for nothing without you.'

I looked at him as though I had never seen him before. He was self-absorbed, selfish, caring only for the pangs and the sufferings of his own heart, and nothing for any others. I saw with clear eyes at last; and then turned away.

'Where are you going?' Sir Edward cried, panic in his voice.

I looked back. 'I am leaving.'

'You cannot! You must not.'

'I can. And I must.'

'*No!*' he shrieked, and caught me by the arm, spinning me round to face him. He gripped my shoulders hard and pulled me close. 'You cannot go. Why would you leave me? Why would you want to?' He stood looking in my face for a moment, then suddenly shook me so violently that I could hear my cogs rattle. '*Why?*' he howled.

I put my hands to his chest and pushed him back, forcing him away from me. 'Tell me, Sir Edward; what is my name?'

He looked at me in utter bewilderment. 'Name?'

'Yes. My name.'

He smiled fondly at me, as one might at a small and foolish child. 'Oh my darling, you don't need a name. You are complete as you are.'

I shook my head. 'You do not know me. You have never known me. You claim to love me, but all you love is your own cleverness reflected in me. I can no longer be a mirror for your vanity, the statue you place on a pedestal and adore simply because it is your statue.'

Sir Edward stared at me, bewildered. 'You're not making sense, my beloved.'

I tried again. 'I cannot sit by with my hands folded while the work of the world goes on, and know nothing of it. What purpose do I serve here, except to be your flatterer and concubine? I have talents, skills I never used while I allowed my existence to be bounded by yours. Shall I let them stagnate in idleness? I must act, I must think, I cannot give these things up now that I have found them.'

If anything, his confusion deepened. 'What are you talking about? What do you want that I do not give you?'

'A cause worthy of my energies. A task to wake me from the stupor I lay under for so many years.'

Sir Edward shook his head. 'I don't understand you.'

I sighed. 'No, you do not. You never will. Let me say something that you can comprehend: I am leaving you. I will not return.'

He stood staring at me for a moment, his face twisting, then suddenly crumpled like a puppet whose strings have been cut. He clutched at my dress, buried his face in my skirts, sobbing wildly. 'Oh, don't leave me, you can't leave, you cannot, I love you – I love you so!' He turned his tear-stained face to look up at me, desperation in his eyes. Then suddenly his gaze sharpened, and he extended a trembling hand. 'Your key! Your key, it's gone. You must have lost it. I'll make you a new one if you stay with me. Oh my darling, you have to stay now! You need me!'

With a sudden pang of terror, I put up my hand to where the key should have hung around my throat. But Sir Edward had spoken the truth. My key had gone. For several long, unbearable, teetering moments, my hands groped desperately over my neck and chest, desperately searching, trying against all logic and sense to believe that the key might have slipped in this direction, in that direction – but it had not. It was not there. It was not there. The key was lost. With a low cry, I pushed Sir Edward from me and turned away, covering my face with my hands in a gesture of utter despair. To live with Sir Edward again. To let myself run down and stutter to a halt. Two insupportable options; and yet it seemed that to one or the other of them I must turn.

I was most completely desolate. My key – I had lost my key. Somehow, in the wild chase across the moors, or when we had been taken and manhandled by the villagers, it had fallen without my noticing – and lacking it, all my vaunted independence of thought was as nothing. For of what use was it to think unaided, when my very existence was dependent on the will of another? I drained the cup of bitterness to its very dregs, then, even cursing that night when I had read the *Vindication* and seen the world open before me; for now, it seemed, that wide, bright world was to be, in one way or another, snatched from me, before I had even begun to explore it. Again I cried out, in the depths of my agony.

'It's all right, my beloved,' Sir Edward said, eagerly, catching me by the hand. 'It's all right, it's not too late, I can make you a new one, we'll be happy again! I'll do it as quickly as I can. When will you next need to wind yourself?'

I started at his words; for they shook loose in me a realisation that had been swamped by my rising panic. 'Last night,' I said, slowly. 'I ought to have wound myself . . . last night.'

Last night, I had sat up and read the *Vindication* until it was almost morning. Last night, my thoughts and sensations had been too fully occupied with the opening vistas I had seen for me to have had any thought to spare for winding myself. Last night, I had gone beyond the time when I should have needed to be wound . . . and had felt no lassitude, no lessening of my ability to move and function, as had always been the case before. Last night . . .

Last night, I had become free.

I drew my hand back from Sir Edward's, and looked him full in the face. 'I no longer require my key, Sir Edward, nor anything else that you can give me. I am independent of you at last.'

His eyes met mine. I saw the colour drain from his face, leaving it as pale as new milk. Then he flung himself to the floor, and crouched against the wall, sobbing bitterly, his hands over his face. I hesitated. His entreaties had not persuaded me, but his despair could still move me. For a moment, I wavered. After all, would it be so terrible to stay – ?

Yes, it would. I could not be the doll he wished to make me, and would only make both of us miserable in the attempt. Leave I must, and leave I would.

'Do not make any more women, Sir Edward,' I said quietly. 'No thinking being can live the life you designed me for.'

I do not know whether he heard me. At any rate, there was no break in the steady rhythm of his sobs, which gradually diminished in volume behind me as I made my way through the corridors.

As I passed through the entrance-hall, a chance glimpse of myself in a mirror on the wall made me turn and look. My hair was matted and dishevelled, my dress torn and dirtied, my slippered feet caked to the ankles in mud. Yet I thought of the well-dressed, perfectly *coiffured* girl who had glided on her smooth path through the days and nights and days of Sir Edward's house, and did not envy her. She had been caged, and I was free. It was the only difference that mattered.

'I am no longer Sir Edward's possession,' I said aloud, my voice echoing in the empty hall. 'I am Dove; and I am ready to fly.'

Then I turned on my heel, and left that house for ever.

There is little more left to tell. As I stood on the steps of the house, wondering where Emily and Lechasseur might have fled to by now, and how on earth I would make contact with them, a terrible thought struck me. Had I, after all, been in time? What if the pursuit of the dogs had outstripped my own attempts to put a stop to them, and my friends had been destroyed even before the housekeeper was? What if –

'Dove!'

I turned, startled, at the cry, to see Emily emerging from the undergrowth. 'Oh, thank God!' I flew down the steps to catch her in a close embrace. 'You are alive! I had feared – '

'It's all right,' she said, clasping me in return. 'It's all right. But Dove,' she added as we pulled apart, 'do you know what happened? Those things were chasing me, and then they just fell over in mid-step and lay there. I came here – I didn't know what else to do, and I thought you or Honoré might be here, maybe. Did you do something?'

I nodded. 'Yes, I did.' I saw her look at me expectantly, but I was not yet ready to talk about my private struggle for freedom, and shook my head. Her look showed that she understood me.

'But where,' I added, 'is – '

'I'm over here,' a quiet voice interrupted, and we turned to see Lechasseur leaning wearily against a tree. There was a long, deep scratch on his face, and one of his sleeves was in tatters.

Emily ran to him. 'Are – are you all right?'

He shrugged. 'Mostly. I had a run-in with a dog. It fell over before it could do much.' He looked at me. 'Was that you?'

I nodded. 'It was me.'

'Thank you,' he said quietly.

It was enough. From a man like him, it was more than enough.

We walked together out of the gates, and I sighed with deep relief. 'I will never go back there again. It is over.'

Lechasseur looked at me quizzically. 'Is it?' he said slowly. 'I'm not sure. I wish I could see – ' He broke off, suddenly, in mid-sentence, still staring at me. There was a long pause, and I had the strangest feeling that he was looking, not *at* me, but *through* me, at something beyond, something only he could see . . . Then he blinked, and seemed to return to himself. 'My God,' he said quietly. 'My God.'

'What is it, Honoré?' Emily asked.

He turned to her. 'It's back, Emily. Her life. Her timeline. It's back.'

'And . . . the important thing?'

He smiled. 'It's there.'

'What is it?' I cut in. 'What are you talking about?'

Lechasseur looked back to me. 'Do you remember when you asked what it was we had to do, and I said that we would know when we'd done it?'

'Yes.'

'Well, it's done.'

I felt a sudden pang. 'Does that mean . . . that you will be leaving?'

'Yes,' Emily said gently, 'I'm afraid so.'

'I wish I could come with you,' I said miserably.

'I'm sorry, but you can't,' Lechasseur told me.

'I know.'

He shook his head. 'No, you don't know. If you came with us, the world we're going back to wouldn't be the same. It wouldn't even exist, not as we know it.'

I frowned. 'I don't understand you.'

'You change the world, Dove,' he said quietly. 'You make a difference.'

I stared at him. 'Truly?'

'Truly.'

'But – how?'

He hesitated. 'I . . . don't think I should tell you too much,' he said slowly. He glanced at Emily, who nodded.

'You see, Dove,' she added, 'if we interfere too much, we might change your timeline again. We don't want to risk that.'

'But could you not at least give me some suggestion?' I pleaded. 'I do not know *how* to change the world.'

'Yes, you do,' Emily told me. 'You just have to *know* that you do.'

I thought about that. Perhaps she was right; but I was still afraid. 'Could you not give me even a small clue?'

Emily and Lechasseur looked at each other. 'Think of that night in the library,' said Lechasseur finally. 'It started then.'

'Thank you,' I said. ' For that assistance. You did not need to give it to me. You have given me so much already. Thank you again, one last time.' I turned back to Emily. 'Thank you, too, for everything. I won't try to keep you from leaving. It is only that I will miss you both.'

She hugged me. 'We'll miss you, too, Dove.'

I clasped her close for a moment. She had been as a sister to me, and if I could, I would have wept to lose her.

When she stepped back, I turned to Lechasseur. He held out his hand, and I shook it. He, I would not embrace. He had courage, persistence, and a dignity not to be trifled with. Much later, when I learned to speak French, I discovered what his name meant, and how well it suited him: Honour, the Hunter.

He extended his hand for Emily to take, but she hung back, looking at me anxiously. 'Dove, I'm worried about you. You said you wouldn't go back to Sir Edward; but where will you go? How will you live?'

I had decided this in my own mind. 'I will return to London, and make my living by writing, as Mary Wollstonecraft did.'

'But are you sure you can support yourself?'

'Yes. I am determined to, and I will do it. I *will* find work.'

Lechasseur stepped forwards. 'Until you do, Dove, take this to tide you over,' and he held out the bag that contained the remains of Sir Richard's money. I began to demur, but he hushed me. 'I won't have any more use for it, and *he* certainly won't. Take it. At the very least, it'll pay your coach fare to London.'

I took the bag. 'Thank you again,' I said. 'I will never forget you both.'

'Goodbye, Dove,' Emily said, a little sadly.

'Goodbye,' Lechasseur echoed.

I only smiled, not trusting myself to speak. The two of them glanced at each other, then clasped hands with each other. There was a moment when their bodies were limned in crackling blue fire . . . a sudden disorientation . . . and they were gone.

I stood still for a long time, staring at the point where they had been, as though I could will them into existence again. But they had gone for good, returned to their mysterious future, and I had never felt so alone.

Then I seemed to hear a quiet voice saying, *Women should . . . think and act for themselves*, and I remembered that I had a cause to fight for, and a mentor to lead me on. I would never be truly alone again. I shook my abstraction from me, and turned my face towards London. There I would go, there I would support myself as a writer, there I would fight for the revolution that Mary Wollstonecraft had called for.

When I hold my hand to my ear and move my fingers, I can hear the whirring of tiny cogs. But we are not constrained by the circumstances of our origin; and if I work hard to secure my independence; if I study to enlarge my mind; if I fight all my days for the cause that I love; then I may, finally, attain a character as a human being, and win myself liberty at last.

They are free, who will be free.

ABOUT THE AUTHOR

Claire Bott is a journalist, currently working full time as a staff writer on *Publishing News* magazine. She used to be a performance poet, before realising there was no money in it and opting to be a hack instead. She quickly found out there was no money in journalism either, but by then she was hooked and it was too late. She wrote for the *Independent*, *Men's Health* and *Comics International* before settling down at *Publishing News*. *The Clockwork Woman* is her first book. About *The Clockwork Woman*, she writes: 'I'm not sure what this book is. An SF retelling of the Pinocchio story; a gender-reversed Frankenstein; a coming-of-age parable; Pygmalion and Galatea with a twist? Anyway, it's got plenty of hairsbreadth escapes, kidnappings and flights over the moors from psychotic robot dogs in it, so that's all right.'

ACKNOWLEDGEMENTS

So many people, so little time. A few of the most important: Clare and Kate, my posse, who provide ever-reliable backup. Dez Skinn, best first boss a person could have. All the old Bunjies crowd, Windmills people especially. Team PN – go guys! Most of all, my parents. Who believe in me even when I've stopped believing in myself.

OTHER TITLES

■ TIME HUNTER ■

A range of high-quality, original paperback and limited edition hardback novellas featuring the adventures in time of Honoré Lechasseur. Part mystery, part detective story, part dark fantasy, part science fiction . . . these books are guaranteed to enthral fans of good fiction everywhere, and are in the spirit of our acclaimed range of *Doctor Who* Novellas.

ALREADY AVAILABLE:

THE WINNING SIDE by LANCE PARKIN

Emily is dead! Killed by an unknown assailant. Honoré and Emily find themselves caught up in a plot reaching from the future to their past, and with their very existence, not to mention the future of the entire world, at stake, can they unravel the mystery before it is too late?
An adventure in time and space.
£7.99 (+ £1.50 UK p&p) Standard p/b ISBN 1-903889-35-9 (pb)

THE TUNNEL AT THE END OF THE LIGHT by STEFAN PETRUCHA

In the heart of post-war London, a bomb is discovered lodged at a disused station between Green Park and Hyde Park Corner. The bomb detonates, and as the dust clears, it becomes apparent that *something* has been awakened. Strange half-human creatures attack the workers at the site, hungrily searching for anything containing sugar . . .

Meanwhile, Honoré and Emily are contacted by eccentric poet Randolph Crest, who believes himself to be the target of these subterranean creatures. The ensuing investigation brings Honoré and Emily up against a terrifying force from deep beneath the earth, and one which even with their combined powers, they may have trouble stopping.

An adventure in time and space.

£7.99 (+ £1.50 UK p&p) Standard p/b ISBN 1-903889-37-5 (pb)

£25.00 (+ £1.50 UK p&p) Deluxe h/b ISBN 1-903889-38-3 (hb)

COMING SOON:

KITSUNE by JOHN PAUL CATTON

In the year 2020, Honoré and Emily find themselves thrown into a mystery, as an ice spirit – *Yuki-Onna* – wreaks havoc during the Kyoto Festival, and a haunted funhouse proves to contain more than just paper lanterns and wax dummies. But what does all this have to do with the elegant owner of the Hide and Chic fashion chain . . . and to the legendary Japanese fox-spirits, the Kitsune?

An adventure in time and space.

£7.99 (+ £1.50 UK p&p) Standard p/b ISBN 1-903889-41-3 (pb)

£25.00 (+ £1.50 UK p&p) Deluxe h/b ISBN 1-903889-42-1 (hb)

PUB: SEPTEMBER 2004 (UK)

TIME HUNTER FILM:

DAEMOS RISING by DAVID J HOWE, directed by KEITH BARNFATHER

Daemos Rising is a sequel to both the *Doctor Who* adventure *The Daemons* and to *Downtime*, an earlier drama featuring the Yeti. It is also a prequel of sorts to Telos Publishing's *Time Hunter* series. It stars Miles Richardson as ex-UNIT operative Douglas Cavendish, and Beverley Cressman as Brigadier Lethbridge-Stewart's daughter Kate. Trapped in an isolated cottage, Cavendish thinks he is seeing ghosts. The only person who might understand and help is Kate Lethbridge-Stewart . . . but when she arrives, she realises that Cavendish is key in a plot to summon the Daemons back to the Earth. With time running out, Kate discovers that sometimes even the familiar can turn out to be your worst nightmare. Also starring Andrew Wisher, and featuring Ian

Richardson as the Narrator.
An adventure in time and space.
£12.00 (+ £2.50 UK p&p) VHS; £14.00 (+ £2.50 UK p&p) DVD
Order direct from Reeltime Pictures, PO Box 23435, London SE26 5WU

■ HORROR/FANTASY ■

URBAN GOTHIC: LACUNA & OTHER TRIPS ed. DAVID J. HOWE
Stories by Graham Masterton, Christopher Fowler, Simon Clark, Debbie
Bennett, Paul Finch, Steve Lockley & Paul Lewis.
Based on the Channel 5 horror series.
SOLD OUT

THE MANITOU by GRAHAM MASTERTON
A 25th Anniversary author's preferred edition of this classic horror novel.
An ancient Red Indian medicine man is reincarnated in modern day New
York intent on reclaiming his land from the white men.
£9.99 (+ £2.50 UK p&p) Standard p/b ISBN: 1-903889-70-7
£30.00 (+ £2.50 UK p&p) Deluxe h/b ISBN: 1-903889-71-5

CAPE WRATH by PAUL FINCH
Death and horror on a deserted Scottish island as an ancient Viking warrior
chief returns to life.
£8.00 (+ £1.50 UK p&p) Standard p/b ISBN: 1-903889-60-X

KING OF ALL THE DEAD by STEVE LOCKLEY & PAUL LEWIS
The king of all the dead will have what is his.
£8.00 (+ £1.50 UK p&p) Standard p/b ISBN: 1-903889-61-8

GUARDIAN ANGEL by STEPHANIE BEDWELL-GRIME
Devilish fun as Guardian Angel Porsche Winter loses a soul to the devil . . .
£9.99 (+ £2.50 UK p&p) Standard p/b ISBN: 1-903889-62-6

ASPECTS OF A PSYCHOPATH by ALISTAIR LANGSTON
Goes deeper than ever before into the twisted psyche of a serial killer.
Horrific, graphic and gripping, this book is not for the squeamish.
£8.00 (+ £1.50 UK p&p) Standard p/b ISBN: 1-903889-63-4

SPECTRE by STEPHEN LAWS

The inseparable Byker Chapter: six boys, one girl, growing up together in the back streets of Newcastle. Now memories are all that Richard Eden has left, and one treasured photograph. But suddenly, inexplicably, the images of his companions start to fade, and as they vanish, so his friends are found dead and mutilated. Something is stalking the Chapter, picking them off one by one, something connected with their past, and with the girl they used to know.

£9.99 (+ £2.50 UK p&p) Standard p/b ISBN: 1-903889-72-3

THE HUMAN ABSTRACT by GEORGE MANN

A future tale of private detectives, AIs, Nanobots, love and death.

£7.99 (+ £1.50 UK p&p) Standard p/b ISBN: 1-903889-65-0

BREATHE by CHRISTOPHER FOWLER

The Office meets *Night of the Living Dead*.

£7.99 (+ £1.50 UK p&p) Standard p/b ISBN: 1-903889-67-7
£25.00 (+ £1.50 UK p&p) Deluxe h/b ISBN: 1-903889-68-5

■ TV/FILM GUIDES ■

BEYOND THE GATE: THE UNOFFICIAL AND UNAUTHORISED GUIDE TO STARGATE SG-1 by KEITH TOPPING

Complete episode guide to the middle of Season 6 (episode 121) of the popular TV show.

£9.99 (+ £2.50 UK p&p) Standard p/b ISBN: 1-903889-50-2

A DAY IN THE LIFE: THE UNOFFICIAL AND UNAUTHORISED GUIDE TO 24 by KEITH TOPPING

Complete episode guide to the first season of the popular TV show.

£9.99 (+ £2.50 p&p) Standard p/b ISBN: 1-903889-53-7

THE TELEVISION COMPANION: THE UNOFFICIAL AND UNAUTHO-RISED GUIDE TO DOCTOR WHO by DAVID J HOWE & STEPHEN JAMES WALKER

Complete episode guide to the popular TV show.

£14.99 (+ £4.75 UK p&p) Standard p/b ISBN: 1-903889-51-0

LIBERATION: THE UNOFFICIAL AND UNAUTHORISED GUIDE TO BLAKE'S 7 by ALAN STEVENS & FIONA MOORE

Complete episode guide to the popular TV show.
Featuring a foreword by David Maloney
£9.99 (+ £2.50 UK p&p) Standard p/b ISBN: 1-903889-54-5

HOWE'S TRANSCENDENTAL TOYBOX: SECOND EDITION by DAVID J HOWE & ARNOLD T BLUMBERG

Complete guide to *Doctor Who* Merchandise.
£25.00 (+ £4.75 UK p&p) Standard p/b ISBN: 1-903889-56-1

■ HANK JANSON ■

Classic pulp crime thrillers from the 1940s and 1950s.

TORMENT by HANK JANSON
£9.99 (+ £1.50 UK p&p) Standard p/b ISBN: 1-903889-80-4
WOMEN HATE TILL DEATH by HANK JANSON
£9.99 (+ £1.50 UK p&p) Standard p/b ISBN: 1-903889-81-2
SOME LOOK BETTER DEAD by HANK JANSON
£9.99 (+ £1.50 UK p&p) Standard p/b ISBN: 1-903889-82-0
SKIRTS BRING ME SORROW by HANK JANSON
£9.99 (+ £1.50 UK p&p) Standard p/b ISBN: 1-903889-83-9
WHEN DAMES GET TOUGH by HANK JANSON
£9.99 (+ £1.50 UK p&p) Standard p/b ISBN: 1-903889-85-5
THE TRIALS OF HANK JANSON by STEVE HOLLAND
£12.99 (+ £2.50 UK p&p) Standard p/b ISBN: 1-903889-84-7

The prices shown are correct at time of going to press. However, the publishers reserve the right to increase prices from those previously advertised without prior notice.

TELOS PUBLISHING c/o Beech House, Chapel Lane, Moulton, Cheshire, CW9 8PQ, England • Email: orders@telos.co.uk • Web: www.telos.co.uk

To order copies of any Telos books, please visit our website where there are full details of all titles and facilities for worldwide credit card online ordering, or send a cheque or postal order (UK only) for the appropriate amount (including postage and packing), together with details of the book(s) you require, plus your name and address to the above address. Overseas readers please send two international reply coupons for details of prices and postage rates.